Not My Sin

A Journey of Survival, Healing, and Hope

Shatha Shanoon

© Copyright 2023 by Shatha Shanoon - All rights reserved.

This document is geared towards providing exact and reliable information regarding the topic and issue covered. The publication is sold with the idea that the publisher is not required to render accounting, officially permitted, or otherwise qualified services. If advice is necessary, legal or professional, a practiced individual in the profession should be ordered.

- From a Declaration of Principles, which was accepted and approved equally by a Committee of the American Bar Association and a Committee of Publishers and Associations.

In no way is it legal to reproduce, duplicate, or transmit any part of this document in either electronic means or in printed format. Recording of this publication is strictly prohibited, and any storage of this document is not allowed unless with written permission from the publisher. All rights reserved.

The information provided herein is stated to be truthful and consistent in that any liability, in terms of inattention or otherwise, by any usage or abuse of any policies, processes, or directions contained within is the solitary and utter responsibility of the recipient reader. Under no circumstances will any legal responsibility or blame be held against the publisher for any reparation, damages, or monetary loss due to the information herein, either directly or indirectly.

Respective authors own all copyrights not held by the publisher.

The information herein is offered for informational purposes solely and is universal as so. The presentation of the information is without contract or any guaranteed assurance.

The trademarks that are used are without any consent, and the publication of the trademark is without permission or backing by the trademark owner. All trademarks and brands within this book are for clarifying purposes only and owned by the owners, not affiliated with this document.

eBook ISBN: 979-8-218-26065-1

Print ISBN: 979-8-218-26039-2

Dedication

I want to dedicate this book to my husband, who supported me and stood by my side all the years. I also dedicate it to my dear friend Kristine Skiff who helped me to be strong and keep writing during difficult times. To all women who are facing terrible times but are still surviving. For the warriors like Hanen, who fight and win by God's blessing.

Contents

Dear Reader

Welcome to the story of Hanen and, ultimately, the story of many Iraqi women. Thank you for choosing to be a part of

Hanen's life by purchasing this book.

The lives of many Iraqi women are not pretty. They experience innumerable horrors, driving many women to believe that good things could never come to them. However, several come to a point where they can look back and see the hand of Allah through it all. I hope you can too.

In way of blessing, "Assalamo alaikum wa rahmatullahe wa barakatohu." *Peace be on you and the mercy and blessings of Allah.*

Thank you again for purchasing this portion of Hanen's life story. I pray you will be blessed and will step away changed in the end.

CHAPTER ONE

The Trigger Red Moon

Present Day, Alberta, Canada

I let my eyelids fall shut and raised my chin to feel the full force of the crisp autumn wind on my face. *Pine.* The wind carried the faint, clean scent from the forests beyond the city.

Spreading my arms, I allowed myself to lean into the stiff breeze as it wrapped its arms around me, pushing back with all its might. I felt alive and free—like I could fly. *Life. That's it, exactly! This place smells and feels like life itself.*

The autumn breeze in Iraq was equally cool and crisp, but it lacked *life*. It never carried the same vibrant, living scent of the air in Alberta.

My smile widened as I turned toward the soft footsteps behind me. Squinting into the dimming light, I could barely make out his figure, but I would know those footsteps anywhere. "Trying to scare me again, were you?" I placed my hands on my hips in mock offense.

As my husband drew nearer, his form blocked the setting sun, and I could see the adoring smile on his face. "I thought since you were dreaming, *Habibti* —" he trailed off as he looked into my eyes.

"I dream only of you, *Amiri.*"

The color rose in his cheeks, flushing them a bright red. A giggle bubbled up within me and spilled out. It never failed to amaze me that, after fifteen years together, I could still make this man blush.

I tussled the edge of my hijab playfully without taking my eyes off his. "Where are you taking me tonight?"

"The Captain's Chair." He paused as he looked over my head at the snow-capped mountains on the horizon before looking back down into my eyes and continuing, "I'm told they serve the best seafood in Edmonton."

"Seafood?" I crossed my arms and tilted my head to the left as I considered this. "But we're hundreds of miles from the ocean. How can they serve seafood here?"

"I imagine they ship it from Vancouver on refrigerated trucks," Akmal's love for sharing new-found facts is shown in the bright sparkle of his eyes and the widening of his smile. His enthusiasm and eagerness to learn were one of the many things that attracted me to him. "If they're punctual with their ordering, they can order the morning before and have the food in time for dinner service the next day."

"That seems like a lot of trouble just so people can eat fish."

Akmal bit the right side of his lower lip while he thought. "I guess it really wouldn't be any different than shipping any other goods," he started slowly, "apart from the need for refrigeration. People ship hand-woven tapestries from Iran to all parts of the world. They ship vases from China to New York and chocolate from Belgium to Buenos Aires. It's a much smaller thing to ship cold food a few hundred miles within the same country."

I nodded and let my hands fall to my side. Pivoting to the north, I took in the lights of the sprawling metropolis surrounding us. "Alberta sure is pretty all lit up at dusk."

"Not half as pretty as you, dear *Hanen*."

A sudden gust of wind cut through my sweater and chilled me, causing a shiver to pass down my spine. Within moments, I felt the warmth of Akmal's arms about me as he draped his flannel jacket over my shoulders. That was another reason I fell in love with my husband; he cared for me more than anyone I ever knew.

I slowly turned toward him again and put on my most flirtatious smile. "Thank you," I whispered close to his ear, "but I'm still cold."

Akmal's grin was heart-warming. "Don't worry," he whispered back. "We'll get you toasty warm soon enough."

My heart began to beat in my ears as I read the desire in his eyes, and I began to feel lightheaded. He'd looked at me like this so many times before. I always enjoyed flirting with my husband. Why was tonight any different?

The station chime sounded. "That's our train," he half-groaned. "I still don't understand why you wanted to take the rail to the restaurant when we have a perfectly good car."

"They don't have trains in Iraq," I tried to cheer him up. "At least not for people. Besides, this is our date night. The whole evening should be special, not just dinner."

"Every evening is special with you, *Habibti*," he said.

I made a show of rolling my eyes and poking his nose, "You're so silly."

"Yes, but you love me anyway."

"I do," I said matter-of-factly and took hold of his hand, rubbing the back of it with my thumb. "I do love you."

Content to simply enjoy one another's company, we didn't speak during the short train ride downtown. Instead, I watched the buildings as they passed. I couldn't believe how clean everything seemed! Edmonton was small compared to Baghdad, but I still expected more rubbish and graffiti.

I shook my head. *After fifteen years in Alberta, you'd think I'd be used to how things are here.* But the opposite was true. I often found myself almost compulsively comparing life in Alberta with my life back home in Iraq.

Home.

I hadn't thought about it until now. But I still thought about Iraq as home. Why? My life was in Alberta now with Akmal, our daughter, and our son. Yet— *Yet I still thought of myself as a visitor…*

"Look!" Akmal shouted suddenly as he shook my shoulder, snapping me out of my reverie.

At first, I stared at him with a stupid look on my face, brow furrowed, lips slightly parted, head cocked, as I tried to figure out what he was trying to say.

"Look!" he repeated with more urgency.

Following his finger, I peered out the train car window and stared at the full moon. It was unlike any moon I'd ever seen before, or at least I thought it was. *Being so large and red, you'd think I'd remember seeing something like it, yet….* I had to have seen something like it because it stirred up a sudden uneasiness within me. It sparked memories I couldn't bring to the surface, feelings I did not wish to explore. And I didn't like that—especially when I didn't know the reason behind it.

"That's called a blood moon," Akmal explained with his typical enthusiasm when recounting some interesting trivia. "It happens during a lunar eclipse when the Earth blocks all sunlight from reaching the moon. The moon appears red because the only light reflected is from the edges of Earth's atmosphere."

"Is today a lunar eclipse?" I tried to make my voice sound normal. I had trouble breathing but couldn't let my husband know. I not only couldn't explain why, but I wouldn't want to worry him tonight of all nights.

"Well, I don't know," Akmal admitted. "Sometimes the moon can seem red if it's low in the sky or if there are dust particles in the atmosphere. It looks fascinating, though."

I looked back up at the moon. It seemed to glow malignantly like a lion's eye staring ominously into my soul. I willed myself to turn away and face the front of the train. Try as I might to block the image of the blood-red eye from my mind, I could still feel its oppressive gaze almost ten minutes later as the train approached our stop.

It didn't take long after disembarking for the fresh, cool breeze to calm my senses. I was smiling and laughing, the red moon forgotten, when a brightly lit sign came into view. It was quite plain, with only the name written upon it. No logo. No symbol. Just big block letters advertising the "Captain's Chair." *So, this is it. An evening in a restaurant with whitewashed walls decorated with anchors, life preservers, and pictures of smiling bearded fishermen proudly standing next to their catch of the year.*

I half-turned as I took the next step to get a better look at my husband's face. His countenance was so bright. He looked at me and smiled, making my heart soar. *At least I'll be with the man of my dreams.*

Stepping inside, the scent of fresh lobster, lemon, and other delicious dishes greeted me. People bustled about quietly. Everything was hushed, no noise above a whisper. I couldn't even hear dishes clanking. *Odd.*

As my eyes adjusted to the dim light, I realized the inside was just as understated as the sign. The décor was subtle and elegant, like the fancy restaurants my dad's family patronized back ho— in Iraq. The staff were dressed similarly, with well-tailored silk shirts, complete with cufflinks and navy-blue coats. I was taken in by the atmosphere of wealth and prominence, fitting for a fine dining establishment.

I gripped Akmal's arm tightly as feelings of nostalgia, unworthiness, and awe hit me simultaneously. I suddenly felt unsteady on my feet. The feeling passed too quickly for Akmal to notice anything was amiss, and we were soon led to our seats near the center of the large dining room.

Akmal glanced around appreciatively. "I have to say, this place feels far classier than I expected."

"I know." I was just as busy taking everything in. "I feel like a princess."

Akmal caught my eye and enraptured me with his mesmerizing smile, "You are my 'amira, my beautiful princess."

I rolled my eyes, trying to stave off the blush I felt warming my cheeks, "You *have* to say that."

"No, I don't. I could be a brute and say terrible things, but then I'd be lying to you. But you are a princess, and I mean it. I could say that to anyone, but I'm saying it to you."

I felt like having some fun. I knew I had Akmal right where I wanted him. I crossed my arms, put both elbows on the table, and leaned in for the kill, "Who else could you say it to?" I narrowed my eyes and pursed my lips.

Akmal blinked, realizing the trap too late. "N—no one!" he stammered. "I'm just saying, I'm calling you a princess because I think you are a princess, not because I feel obligated to."

I suppressed the smile wanting to push itself on my lips. This was more fun than I thought it would be! "Would you call any other woman a princess?"

"No!" Akmal protested. "I just—" That's when I started sputtering and giggling. I couldn't hold it in any longer. He sighed and shook his head. "You know what? Fine!" he said, blushing and grinning. "You're not a princess. You're a brat; that's what you are."

I broke down and burst out into full-fledged belly laughter. Akmal joined me, unable to keep up the pretense of frustration anymore. "A man tries to say something nice to his wife…" he said, smiling and shaking his head. I, on the other hand, couldn't stop giggling.

However, it didn't take long for me to realize people were staring at us. Scooping up the cloth napkin from under my silverware, I nearly caused my utensils to crash to the floor. My quick reflexes saved them just in time, and I placed them on my plate. *Too loud…* and cleared my throat behind my napkin.

Oh no! What must Akmal be thinking? I bit my lip. *Is he offended? Or, worse, embarrassed? Had I embarrassed him?* I slowly lifted my eyes to glance his way. The fake-annoyed look Akmal had pasted on his face triggered another fit of laughter from us both.

The sound of a male clearing his throat stopped our chuckling cold. Startled, I gasped and nearly jumped out of my seat.

"May I take your order, please?" the waiter asked politely.

"Oh, yes! Of course." Akmal flashed another smile my way before ordering for us both. On the other hand, I hid behind the menu until the waiter asked me to hand my menu to him. Now, I had nothing to hide behind. I decided to behave.

We weren't disappointed with the food. As promised, my braised halibut was delicious, and Akmal raved about his lobster with butter sauce. *Fresh seafood? And nearly a thousand miles from the nearest ocean. Nigh impossible. But…* My life is so much like the food we ate. It was beautiful, fulfilling, and deliciously sweet, and, like the fish so far from the ocean, it didn't seem possible.

We spent the remainder of the evening talking, laughing, and teasing one another like schoolchildren. Occasionally, I would find myself simply watching Akmal as he ate. I couldn't help but marvel that I could have found someone so perfect for me. Or, rather, that my parents could have found someone so perfect. That was the true marvel.

Once, he caught me staring. He smiled and blushed again—*Oh, how I love when he blushes!* —and asked, "What are you looking at?"

"Only you, *Amiri,*" I replied.

Setting his fork down, he gathered his cloth napkin and wiped the corners of his mouth. "Shall we?" Standing from his seat, he offered his hand.

"I'd be delighted, I'm sure," I teased, trying to sound just as proper and prim. We both chuckled again before marching off to pay the bill.

Because neither of us wanted the night to end, we left the "Captain's Chair" and began walking toward a nearby park. Because he was familiar with the area, Akmal knew it had brightly lit walking trails and that there would be plenty of others walking them. However, they wouldn't be too crowded because of the time of night.

Knowing my fear of dark, desolate places where one could easily be mugged, raped, or worse, he quickly pointed out all the perks. Making a great show of taking a deep breath and blowing it out slowly, I made a face like I was thinking hard about going to the park, where dark, dangerous people might lurk. The truth was that I felt safe going, given all the information, but I wanted to tease him a bit first. "Mmmm… Yeahhh… I guess. Under one condition."

"What's that?"

"I get to hold onto you all the way."

He smiled down at me, "Forever and always."

I gently laced my arm through Akmal's elbow when he offered it, and he led me down a soft path that wound through rolling fields of grass dotted with plots of geraniums and daylilies. Later, as we strolled through towering aspen and pine stands, I breathed in a cleansing breath of the cool night air. Though it was cooler than it had been at dusk, the breeze was softer, so the night air wasn't as chilling. I imagined that the breeze was caressing my cheeks with soft fingers.

"Hamsa and Hamid are growing so quickly," Akmal sighed. "It won't be too many years , and she will be going to University," he said as he reminisced about his job and our children while we walked.

I turned my eyes toward Akmal's face and nodded in agreement. Hamid was home with my friend, Allisa. *He should be bedding down soon.*

I allowed my gaze to shift up to the bright moon, no longer red and glowering, as I listened to the deep baritone of his voice. I loved the sound of his voice. *I could lose myself in those deep notes.* I breathed a silent prayer of thanks for granting me this beautiful moment in a beautiful place with the man I loved.

"Look here." Akmal had paused us before a small pond. The beauty of the moonlight gleaming off the pond's surface, casting a soft, silver glow on everything, took my breath away.

"Amazing—" It came out as a whisper so soft that I was certain it was lost on the breeze.

I felt, more than saw Akmal move closer to me and begin staring at me. Turning toward Akmal, I smiled up into his beautiful eyes. My husband gazed down at me with the purest expression of love I had ever seen, although I imagined he had looked upon me that way many times. Lifting a hand, he softly caressed my cheek. Though he was surprised by this show of public affection, I placed my hand over his.

"You are so beautiful, *my pure Hanen. May Allah keep you beside me for all my life.*"

My heart suddenly sped up, even as it jumped into my throat. My palms began to sweat, and my whole body felt weak. When he spoke to me with his face hovering so close to mine, the scent of his breath filled my nostrils. It wasn't bad, a little sour from the lobster and the madeleines we'd enjoyed for dessert, but not bad. Nonetheless, it sent a wave of revulsion through me. I turned away, suddenly nauseous.

"What's wrong?" Akmal asked, concerned.

"I don't... I, umm..." I searched for the words, but they wouldn't form around the lump in my throat. He reached for me, and I instinctively withdrew from his touch. I felt lightheaded and weak, and nausea churned my stomach until I turned toward the pond and retched.

"Hanen!" I heard Akmal cry out.

His arms were around me instantly, steadying me so I didn't fall into the water. His touch made my skin crawl, and I tried to pull away again, but I was too weak to move. I retched again. Akmal moved my hijab to the side where it was creeping up my cheek, threatening to spill over my shoulder. He steadied me until the nausea passed, and I could stand again.

"Hanen!" Akmal cried again. "Talk to me! What's going on? Are you okay?"

I took a deep breath, allowing the cool air to calm my roiling stomach. It did nothing to calm my racing thoughts. All I could manage was a nod in response to his question.

"Is everything okay?" I heard a strange voice ask. I looked up to see another couple approaching us, concern written on their faces.

How embarrassing…

"I'm fine," I managed to weakly thank them. "I…" I didn't want to embarrass Akmal any further than I must have already. "Something I ate must not have agreed with me."

Akmal led me away from the pond. "Let's get you home. I'll call a cab."

I nodded again. I kept my head down, ashamed, and allowed Akmal to guide me down the path back to the street. His touch still made my flesh crawl, and I had to fight hard to avoid vomiting again. By the time we reached the street, my nausea had calmed enough that I could sit in the taxi without feeling dizzy. I was pleasantly surprised when Akmal reached over and caressed my forehead, and my skin no longer crawled with revulsion.

A rush of guilt flooded me, replacing the nausea, and tears filled my eyes. "I'm so sorry." My words were so soft that, at first, I wasn't sure if he had heard me.

Akmal pursed his lips and tilted his head. "Enough of that," he whispered. "Let's get you home and get you some rest."

I looked at my hands, folded neatly in my lap, trying to hold back the torrent of tears. I knew if they started, they wouldn't stop. Too many memories. Too many regrets. But the evening had been so wonderful, and things were going so well. It had been years since I'd panicked like this. *Why, tonight of all nights, did I have to break down like that? What must Akmal think of me?*

"I'm sorry, Love," I whispered more loudly. "I just felt sick suddenly. Maybe the fish…."

"Hush, Dear," Akmal insisted gently. "Let's just get you home so I can care for you."

The cab driver was staring dutifully at the road, but I could see his eyes in the rearview mirror. There was disapproval there. And why not? I deserved it. Akmal had been nothing but kind to me since we met. He was kind and gentle and loving and strong. He provided a wonderful home for our children and me and respected me in the way a good husband should. I called him Amiri—my prince—and that's exactly what he was. *How could I possibly compare him to—*

Another wave of nausea ran through me, and I retched but managed not to vomit. Instantly Akmal's arms were around me. That should have comforted me, but instead, it repelled me as his closeness had at the water. Instinctively, I shoved him away. He fell backward, shock, hurt, and concern evident on his face.

"I'm so sorry, Akmal," I could feel how wide my eyes were and how the blood had drained from my face. I imagined I was more pale than normal, though he could not see that now as dark as it was in the cab. "I don't know what's wrong with me."

The shock and hurt disappeared from his face, leaving only concern. "Maybe we should take you to the hospital," he said. "You seem really ill." He turned to the cab driver and instructed him to divert to the hospital.

"No!" I cried. "No hospital. I just need to rest. It's just something I ate."

Akmal considered me dubiously. "If you're in this much pain and don't know what's wrong, we should have someone look at you."

Even now, his only thought was for me. Tears came to my eyes once more. *He spent so much time planning this evening and tried so hard to make it special for me, and this is how I repay him?*

"I'm so sorry," a tear escaped the corner of my eye.

"That's enough!" he said sternly. The cab driver glanced behind him briefly but said nothing. Akmal continued more gently. "You have nothing to be sorry for. You didn't cook the food, did you?"

I didn't look at him. Instead, I stared at my hands. But I did shake my head.

"Well then, why would you be sorry? Let's get you home and in bed."

It's not the food… But I couldn't say that aloud. *It's not the food; it's… I felt his hot breath on me, its scent filling my nostrils. It wasn't bad, a little sour from the laban, but not terrible. Still, it sent a wave of revulsion through me, and I…*

I couldn't open the cab window quickly enough, but finally, I stuck my head out the window. The rush of cold air shocked me out of my thoughts and drove away the nausea that threatened once more to overwhelm me.

"Hanen!" Akmal cried.

He grabbed me by the waist. It was then that I realized with relief that his touch no longer repelled me. I slumped back in my seat and rolled the window up.

"It's okay, *Amiri*," I sighed. "I feel better now."

We reached our house a few minutes later. I felt better, but Akmal insisted on helping me up the front steps.

When we entered the front door, Allisa sat on the couch helping Hamsa and Hamid with their homework. She stood up slowly and walked toward us. "You two are back early. Hey, did you guys see the moon earlier? It was…" She broke off when she saw my face. "What's wrong?"

"Something she ate," Akmal explained. "Do you mind staying a few more minutes until I get Hanen settled in bed?"

"Of course," Allisa said. "Is everything okay?"

"She's a little sick, but she'll be okay," Akmal said. "She just needs to rest."

"What happened?" Allisa asked, her rising concern evident in the high pitch of her voice. Hamsa and Hamid looked up to see what was happening. "Was there a problem with the food?"

I nodded but couldn't bring myself to look her in the face. Allisa had a way of knowing when I was lying, and I didn't want to risk that Allisa would try to dig for the truth.

"Why don't you tell the kids to shower, and then you can go home after that?" Akmal offered.

"Not a chance!" Allisa declared. "I'm going to stay and help. I'll ensure the kids finish their homework, have showers, and go to bed. Right now, I'm going to make some peppermint tea. You'll like it, Hanen. It's soft and soothing and great for nausea."

"Thank you," Akmal said. "I'll pay you an extra hour for your trouble."

Allisa's brow furrowed. "Pay me? You're not paying me anything! I'm your friend, I don't work for you. Hanen, tell him he's not paying me anything."

A soft smile turned up my lips, but I didn't say anything. I still didn't want to risk looking Allisa in the eye.

"You, poor dear," Allisa said. "You really are in pain. Akmal, go take care of her and let me worry about the children. And if I see you reach for your wallet even once, I'll never speak to you again."

Akmal helped me upstairs and led me to our bedroom. I let him tuck me into the bed and fluffed the pillows. "Are you comfortable?" He was so sweet and kind.

"I'm fine. Thank you, Love." I forced a smile that I hoped seemed genuine.

Akmal returned a warm smile of his own, then headed back downstairs.

After he left, I glanced at the picture of Hamsa, Hamid, and me on the nightstand. It was then that I saw the candles tucked behind it. Akmal worked so hard to plan this night and make it special for us both. I wanted so much to enjoy it with him. *Why, tonight, of all nights, did I have to remember my uncle?*

Akmal and Allisa returned with a tray holding a cup of peppermint tea and a glass of water.

Akmal cleared the nightstand, trying to hide the candles from my view as he did so. Another rush of guilt overwhelmed me. "Akmal, Love, I'm so sorry I ruined tonight."

"Hush, *Habibti*," he chided gently, "I already told you that you have nothing to be sorry for. Any night with you is beautiful. Just rest and drink your tea. I will walk Allisa outside, and then I'll be back to check on you."

"I don't mind staying," Allisa said.

"It's okay," I told her. "I feel much better already. I just need to rest. I'll be fine in the morning. Thank you, Allisa."

Allisa didn't seem entirely happy, but she allowed Akmal to lead her out of the room.

I sipped my peppermint tea slowly. The brew was warm and cleansing. Soon, my nausea faded and then disappeared completely.

My thoughts, though, were a different story altogether. My mind kept returning to our time by the pond. Then it wandered back to the memories that overwhelmed me when I smelled the scent of my dear husband's breath, just as the lake's water would have engulfed me if I had fallen in. *Oh, that it had. Then, these memories wouldn't torment me!*

I wanted nothing more than to sleep and forget, but sleep wouldn't come. So, I lay awake staring at the ceiling, remembering.

CHAPTER TWO

Fatherhood Bonding

5 years old, Baghdad, Iraq

"H's tired all the time," My mother's hand stopped mid- chop, and her eyes darted toward Shameera and me, where we played with our dolls on the floor.

"Lana!" Grandmother Khadja hushed her in a frantic yet chiding tone, "The children!"

Mother raised her eyebrows slightly and started to open her mouth but snapped it shut and continued chopping her carrots. After a moment, she looked up again at her. "He barely sees his children anymore. I don't expect him to dote on us all day, but is it too much to ask that he share a meal with us occasionally?"

I listened hard, but it took a few minutes for my five-year-old brain to realize they were talking about Father. My face brightened. *Father!* But my smile faded as quickly as it had appeared. Mother was right. I didn't get to see Father very often, and he was always exhausted when I *did* get to see him.

"The men work. The women cook," Grandmother reprimanded forcefully without looking up from stirring her soup. "That's the way it is. It is not our place to be ungrateful for what Allah has given us in this life."

Mother's jaw tightened, and the knuckles on her chopping hand turned white, but she said nothing. Grandmother's word was law, and once she'd spoken about a subject, there was nothing else to say.

"We have too much to do today to worry about trivial matters anyway," Grandmother's voice was softer, almost apologetic. "Midnight will usher in the eve of Ashura!"

I knew what that meant. Baghdad had already grown busier as masses of black-clad Arba'een pilgrims en route to Karbala began pouring in the gates earlier that morning. Tomorrow morning would bring more pilgrims, but that did not excite me. The day before Ashura, the ninth day of Muharram, marked the day Baghdad shifted into action! Sure, there would be fun to be had, but what enthralled me the most were the big pots that fed the masses. And what's more, Father would be cooking lamb and qeema in those pots! And that meant Father would be—

"Father!" Shameera's shrill squeal jarred me from my thoughts.

Father? "Father!" my squeal matched hers, tone for tone, as I threw my doll half across the room and jumped to my feet. Racing to Father as quickly as my legs would carry me, I joined Shameera, hugging Father's free leg tightly. "Oh! Father!"

"And there's my little piece of Heaven!" I always loved hearing Father's smile in his voice, even when he was so tired. I turned to see Bayza toddling into the kitchen, her thumb in her mouth and her stuffed kitten tucked under her arm.

"Momma, Zayna, wake me up." Oblivious to the excitement, Bayza stuck her thumb right back into her mouth and laid her head on Mother's lap.

Mother rubbed circles on Bayza's back and turned to look at Father. He looked sad and dejected. Mother just shrugged. Did she really not care?

"It's okay, Father," Shameera took his right hand in her left and looked lovingly into his eyes. "Bayza's still three. When she's not tired anymore, she'll see you're here. Then she'll be happy too! Just like us!"

Father's smile returned to his face, but it didn't quite reach his eyes, and his sadness touched my heart.

Suddenly, Zayna's piercing cry split the awkward silence.

Mother's head and shoulders fell forward, and she ran her hand through her hair. "Well, that was the shortest break I've ever put in," she sighed loudly. Using the table to push herself to her feet, she looked in our direction, "Shameera, set the table. Bayza, sit here and wait for Momma and Hanen—"

"Hanen will help me with the soup," Grandmother interrupted.

Mother's jaw tightened again. She was displeased at Grandmother's interference. I'd heard Mother tell Father before that he needed to stand up to Grandma and remind her whose children we were, but Father would never do that. I knew that. Mother knew that, and so did Grandmother. So, things continued and would continue, just like they always had. Grandmother had spoken, and no one else had a say.

As Mother pivoted on her heel to march toward her screaming four-month-old, Father peeled Shameera and me off his sides and hurried toward her. "Wait," he implored. "Let me."

Mother stopped midstride, her back still to him. Her hands were balled into fists, and her knuckles turned white momentarily. Finally, she relaxed her hands, crossed her arms, and turned toward him. She still didn't look him in the eye. "Well?" she snapped impatiently.

Father's brow furrowed as he looked at her questioningly. "She's still screaming…." Mother waved one hand toward the

nursery. "Never mind. I'll—"

"No!" Father jumped into action. "I'm sorry. I'm just… I… I'll get her." Father disappeared around the corner, and I soon heard his gentle voice speaking to my baby sister.

"Men," Mother said the one word like it was the reason for all the world's problems.

"Shameera, stop doting and set the table, Dear."

***

I stirred ever so carefully under my blankets. The sun was just starting to cast a hint of pale orange glow on the tip-top of the windowsill. *What woke me?* I peered over at the alarm clock sitting on the floor beside me. *4:57 a.m.*

"Praise is to Allah, Who gives us life after He has caused us to die, and to Him is the return," Father's soft voice was comforting. "Praise is to Allah, Who gave strength to my body, returned my soul to me, and permitted me to remember Him." Father was performing Fajr and reciting his dua for waking.

I had asked Father once what the dua meant. "What does it mean; cause us to die and to Him is the return?'" I had asked.

"Well," he had explained, "there are two forms of death. We die when we leave this life and go to Jannah or Jahannam, but while we live, anytime we sleep, we enter a temporary death. During real death, Allah sends the good souls to Jannah and the bad souls or those who committed shirk to Jahannam. But at the end of temporary death, sleep, Allah releases our souls back to us until an appointed time."

I nodded. Now the dua all made sense. "Praise is to Allah, Who gives us life after He has caused us to die, and to Him is the return." I tried to be respectful and reverential, but I could feel Father watching me. I was itching to hug his neck and talk to him about the day's activities.

Standing from my mat, I found Father in my doorway, right where I expected him to be. Running to him, I jumped into his arms. He swung me into the air before hugging me tight, and I planted kisses on both of his cheeks. "Can I help today, Father? May I help too?"

Father's brow furrowed for a moment, as it always does when he's thinking. "I'm not sure, Hanen. Let me check with your mother."

"But, Father," I whined. "She'll say, No…."

Father chuckled and hugged me tightly once more. "How about you come to get breakfast with me. Mother is downstairs. She has it prepared already. I can smell it." Father made a big scene of sniffing the air, "I smell… I smell… Hmm. What *do* I smell?"

"Eggs!" I offered. "Yes! Eggs. And rice!"

"And I think, maybe, tomato?"

Father tickled me under my chin and chuckled. I giggled at his antics. "Perhaps!" Setting me down beside him, he took my hand, and we started down the steps together, father and daughter, to meet the day.

Exiting the staircase, we turned right and right again and immediately found ourselves in the kitchen. Father and I both stopped in our tracks and gaped in awe at Mother. She stood like a proper lady should, head straight up, back straight. Everything was perfect.

And her outfit. Her long skirt was dark like the depths of the unsearchable sea. And her ruffled blouse was green. Allah's favorite color. She wore a wide braided belt, which accentuated her thin waist. She hadn't donned her Hijab yet, as it was only our family in the house, so her long black hair fell in tight curls to the small of her back. The sides were fashionably pinned back with her ivory clips. She looked like a queen of heaven.

As she opened the oven to take the biscuits out, the escaping air blew a loose strand of hair into her face. She turned her face slightly our way. Her cheeks were rosy from the heat. *So beautiful!* Maybe she *was* a queen of heaven!

Mother was startled as she caught sight of us out of the corner of her eye. Embarrassed by the attention, she giggled and ran her fingers through her hair. "What…?"

Father let my hand drop and glided toward Mother. He took one of her hands and looked into her eyes, "We're just looking at the beauty that is you, *Habibti.*"

Mother's smile was wide, but only briefly before she waved him away. "Oh, you speak such foolery, Ayad. You know those who lied will have black faces on the Day of Judgment." She started to turn toward the stove, but Father tenderly touched her shoulder to gently turn her back toward him.

"No, dear Lana. Those who lied about Allah will have black faces out of shame. I am not lying about Allah."

Mother's eyes were large and bright. She raised her finger and opened her mouth to speak, "Aha—"

"Nope!" Father put his hand in the air to stop Mother from speaking. "Neither am I lying to you."

***

Come 6 a.m., Father and I were standing before a small, recently built fire. The relentless sun was rising higher and beginning to burn through the grey morning fog that shrouded the sky.

"Step back," Father gently pressed me back from the fire with his palm as he stepped toward it, a jug of some sort and a thick, pointed stick in the other.

"What's that, Father?"

"Kerosene. After I add some firewood to the small sticks and embers, I will pour a bit on the fire. It should make it catch well and burn hot."

I smiled. *Father knows so much!*

After almost ceremoniously placing the wood on the fire under the big aluminum pot, Father poured a little kerosene from the oddly shaped jug into a red plastic cup and replaced the lid on the jug. Looking back over his shoulder, he waved me back further. Satisfied, he smiled, turned, and threw the foul-smelling liquid on the fire.

As soon as the kerosene met the hungry flames, they grew so intense that the heat pushed me backward. "Father!" but Father sat crouched where he was, unmoving.

"I love looking at fire, Hanen. It reminds me of the depths of Allah's love for us. It's a burning love. A kind love. A merciful and forgiving love. In fact, sometimes, we may make mistakes, but if we ask honestly for forgiveness and do not repeat those sins, Allah will forgive us! So great is His love."

Standing up, Father smiled at me, put his large right hand on his hip, and cocked his head. I could tell the time for seriousness was over. "Well? Are we ready to cook some garbanzo beans?"

A smile broke across my face as I nodded my head.

Father smiled in return. He began ladling the beans into the pot from the large vat near it. "This handy ladle is called a chifcheer," he told me proudly. "These beans will cook all day long. Later, we'll beat the beans into a paste. Then, we'll add shredded lamb and onion to make the qeema that we have every year!"

Father's face changed to one of concern. "Hanen? Are you alright?"

"Yes, Father." I bit my lip and crossed my ankles but quickly uncrossed them when I almost fell. *I waited too long!* I turned to run inside but called over my shoulder, "I'm sorry, Father! I have to go!"

Minutes later, after the emergency had passed, I was on my way back outside. Passing the closed kitchen door, I heard Mother's voice inside, "Ah! Careful!", she squealed so loudly and with authority and such fear at the same time that it scared me! *What? Is she hurt?* "Mother?" I shoved through the door. "Mo—"

Mother and Grandmother stood near the sink. They stared at me with their eyes wide and their mouths hanging open. They turned their heads to look down between them simultaneously. Each of them held two legs of a headless animal. It had no skin, head, or hooves, but I could tell what it was.

Mother found her voice and started shaking her head, "No… Hanen…" Her voice was low and filled with emotion.

Suddenly, Grandmother kicked into action. I watched half the lamb fall toward the floor as she dropped the two legs she was clutching. I felt Grandmother kneel beside me. "Hanen, Beloved?" But I couldn't tear my eyes away from the lamb to look her way. "Hanen, look at Grandmother."

Slowly, I turned toward Grandmother, but I couldn't meet her eyes. Instead, I stared into the depths of the evil eye pin that Grandmother wore on the shoulder of her beige shrug.

"Hanen?" Mother was kneeling at my other side.

"You weren't—"

As my eyes traveled back to the lamb, now lying half in the sink and half on the counter, the tears began to flow. I saw Grandmother rush to the sink and wash her hands, but she was quickly back at my side and pulling me into her arms.

"Hanen!" I heard the alarm in Father's voice. "Mother, what happened?" I heard the fall of his footsteps as he rushed toward me.

"She'll be okay," Grandmother hugged me. "She saw the lamb for the evening meal."

"The lamb! But the children shouldn't... She's so young!" I felt Father gently take me from Grandmother's arms. I burrowed my face into his chest and breathed in his scent and the comfort that was only Father.

He carried me upstairs to my room, laid me on my mat, and covered me. "Take your rest, Sweet Hanen. You'll feel better in a bit."

Then he left me to my dreams, where I was chased by skinless, headless lambs until I fell headlong into the bottomless depths of the dark blue evil eye.

CHAPTER THREE

Sour Sweet Memories

"Hanen," Mother was rubbing circles on my back. I slowly opened my eyes. They felt heavy with sleep. *What time is it?* Turning onto my side, I looked toward the window. *Sunrise?*

"The fun and celebrations of Ashur are starting. I didn't want you to miss out."

Sunset? Had I slept all day? Then I remembered. Groaning, I clutched my stomach. I suddenly felt nauseous. I remembered the lamb. The skinless, headless lamb. It all came flooding back. Soon, the feeling passed. "Why, Mother? Why did you?" I felt a tear trace down my cheek. Then, another. Sitting on the floor beside me, Mother pulled me into her lap and let me cry into her bosom until I was through.

"Oh, Beloved! We didn't kill that lamb. Is that what you thought?"

I nodded my head and looked up into her face. Using her thumb, she traced the path of my tears down my cheek.

"No, Hanen. I could never kill such an innocent creature."

"But you—" I suddenly remembered what Grandmother had said, "*She saw the lamb for the evening meal.*" I began to sob again.

"Come, my child. Let's go get you cleaned up. Then you can play with the other children."

I didn't feel like playing. I didn't feel like doing anything, but I also didn't feel like arguing with Mother, not when I didn't have

Grandmother near to back me up. I slid my hand into Mother's and obediently followed her downstairs.

Mother continued to talk while she washed my face and pulled back my hair.

Though I heard her speaking, I didn't hear the words until she said Makhi's name. I perked up. "Makhi?" I repeated.

"Yes. All of your uncles are here. They came to help Father with the qeema. Makhi has been asking after you."

I loved spending time with Makhi. He wasn't like my other uncles, who were boring, old, and traditional. He was funny, always making jokes, and easy to talk to. He was 11 years older than me, but we were really close. We'd play games together in our tarma—like football and marbles. And he'd buy me ice cream, which we'd eat together as we sat on the swing at their house and talked. Yes, Makhi was my favorite of all the uncles. I rushed to finish getting ready. I wanted to get outside with Makhi.

"You seem to be feeling better."

I shrugged my shoulders and peeked at mother with a half-smile on my face. I figured I'd never get that poor lamb's image out of my head. I didn't know if I'd ever be able to put another bite of it in my mouth. But visiting with Makhi would make me feel better in any situation.

Mother's face lit up. "Good." She kissed my forehead and turned me toward the bathroom door, patting me on the behind, "Go on and play."

Walking out the front doors and onto the tarma, I inhaled deeply. The aroma of qeema cooking over the open fires mixed splendidly with the sweet scent of the flower gardens to the left and right of the cobblestone path I stood on. But then I thought of the lamb in the qeema—the lamb I'd seen in our kitchen, and my stomach began to churn. I swallowed hard once, then twice, around the lump in my throat. I focused on the soft, cool breeze blowing on my face and the wind rustling through the tops of the few palm trees inside the tarma. Soon, the feeling passed.

"Hanen!" Makhi came dancing through one of the cast iron gates at the other end of the tarma, a large smile pasted on his face. "How is my favorite girl tonight?" he sang. "Girl! We are going to have fun tonight! Food, games, reading the Ziyara and Quran, and prayer!"

His energy was contagious, and soon, my smile matched his. Grabbing my hand, he led me toward the gate. "But Makhi? I'm not to leave the tarma," I said apprehensively. *Surely, he knows that.*

Picking me up, he swung me around and hugged me tightly. "Oh, beloved Hanen, don't you remember? It's the eve before Ashur! Everyone is out in the streets! The men are cooking qeema, and the children are playing!"

"But not Mother and Grandmother?"

I always played soccer with Makhi and the others inside the tarma, but this was different. This game had big kids in it. Kids much bigger than me. And they wouldn't be careful with me. "I don't know." I took a step backward.

"Oh! No! They have their duties inside!" He set me back down. "You are getting so big, Beloved!" He placed his hand under my chin and pulled my face upward so he could look into my eyes. "Yes. So big indeed."

Taking my hand once more, he winked at me. I did my best to wink at him. "Ready?"

I nodded and smiled. "Perfect."

Leaving the tarma, I saw Father out by his aluminum pot. "There are so many pots now! More than there were this morning! There must be hundreds!"

"No, Beloved. Maybe 50, perhaps 60, or 65. But not hundreds." He smiled down at me.

Suddenly, the loud talking that came from the direction where the men were seated quieted. Curious, I watched them rise simultaneously and remove the lids from their pots. Picking up the large sticks leaning against their pots, they flipped them over and began to stir their qeema. After a few moments, they returned their sticks, replaced their lids, and sat back down. The talking began again. *Interesting.*

"It never fails to amaze me. Almost ceremonial." Makhi's tone was quiet and reverent. Pulling my hand, he pressed me to move toward the group of children in the street.

At first, I couldn't tell what they were doing, but as we drew closer, it became evident. A small group of children were cheering while two other groups of children were battling over the soccer ball between them. Suddenly, a short-haired boy wearing a black skull cap kicked the ball to his teammate between another boy's legs. A girl intercepted, drove the soccer ball to the end of the field, and sank it into the net.

"Goal!" Makhi's shout rang out loud and clear.

The team ran together and hoisted the girl who made the winning shot on their shoulders. Several of them gave her high fives. The other team ran up to her as well. "Great job!" they offered. "Great game!"

"Do you want to join in the next one?" Makhi had seen the intrigue in my eyes.

"You'll do great!"

I looked up at Makhi, "Do you really think so?"

"Would I lie to you?"

"No. Never." Smiling, I let go of his hand and rushed toward the group.

"Let's play marbles!" they yelled. "Yeah! Marbles!" Then they all ran off in the other direction, leaving me alone in the street.

Lowering my head, I felt a tear trickle down my cheek. I wiped it off with the back of my hand. *No. Not today. I've cried too much already. I will be strong.*

I felt a hand on my shoulder. Turning, I saw Makhi behind me. "I'm here." He was always there when I needed him. He would always be there.

A smile toyed with the corner of my lips. "I love you, Makhi."

"I love you, Beloved. And I always will. Say, you've had a rough day. How about an ice cream?"

I nodded my head.

"Let's go ask your father."

I took Makhi's hand and allowed him to lead me to Father's pot. "Ayad?"

Father looked up at us.

"Hanen has had a very hard day. I believe ice cream would make her feel better."

Father thought for a moment. "Perhaps…" "I want to take her to get ice cream."

"On your bicycle?" questioned Father. "Yes. On my bike."

Father's brow wrinkled as he thought again. "I don't know, Makhi. It doesn't seem very safe.…"

"But it is! I've never fallen from my bike." "Oh, just let the girl go."

Father startled, "Mother! I didn't see you there!"

"Of course not. I am invisible unless I'm needed," Grandmother huffed. "Let Hanen go. She'll only be young once."

"Yes, mother."

I smiled widely. I was going to ride on a bike! Better than that, I was going to ride Makhi's bike! With Makhi!

"Oh! Thank you, Grandmother!" I turned to run after Makhi, who was already walking toward his bike. Turning again, I yelled back, "Thank you, Father!"

Father half-smiled and waved goodbye.

"Hold on tight," Makhi told me after he helped me climb on the back of his bicycle.

I nodded my head and hugged his back tight. As he pedaled, I tightened my grip and pressed my cheek into his back.

The ride was much too short as we pulled to a stop before the ice cream shop, and Makhi helped me down. "Get anything you want."

"Anything?"

Makhi nodded his head. "They have food too. I heard you might want something other than qeema tonight. They have rice, roast beef, and broccoli. Does that sound good?"

My mouth began to water, and it was my turn to nod. My belly audibly growled, causing us both to laugh.

"Well, we better not keep *that* waiting! It's liable to eat your backbone!" Makhi chuckled, and I giggled as we walked into the shop.

The meal was delicious. It was almost too much for me to eat between that and the chocolate ice cream cone. Almost. I groaned while Makhi was helping me onto the back of his bike.

"Did I feed you too much?"

"Oh! No!" I quickly assured him, but I had to keep myself from groaning with each bump on the way back to the festivities.

The rest of the night was splendid. I didn't want to play with the other children, so Makhi played football with me and various games with the marbles in the tarma until I was too tired to stay awake any longer. "I must go to bed, Makhi."

"I guess it is getting late. It's nearly midnight. They'll begin reading the Quran and praying soon." I knew he'd be joining that and the reading of the Zayara anyway. "Should I come to tuck you in?"

I didn't want Makhi to miss out on the fun, but I also didn't want to miss any special time with him. It was so hard to choose! "Only if you want to…." I looked down at the toe of my shoe, which I used to bore a hole in the dirt.

Makhi was silent for a moment. A cloud of despair began to overshadow me. *He doesn't want to.* "Want to? Of course, I want to! I want to spend all the time in the world with you!"

"Really?" I looked up into Makhi's smiling face and barely kept myself from jumping for joy. "Oh! Thank you, Makhi!" I squealed.

Climbing the stairs toward my bedroom, I listened to Makhi talk of a beautiful place he had found in the brush off the side of the road out in the middle of nowhere. He said there was a spring there. "I'll take you there one day," he promised.

I tried to hide a yawn with my hand. "I'm sorry, Makhi. I don't mean to be rude."

"Don't worry, Beloved. I didn't think anything of it. Here's your mat."

Lying down, I tucked my feet up under my blankets. Makhi pulled them the rest of the way over me and brushed his thumb over my cheek. "Sleep sweet."

"Makhi?" Grandmother stuck her head in the door.

"I was just putting Hanen to bed," he sounded almost defensive.

"Um. Okay?" Grandmother rubbed the back of her neck. "The men are about to begin. They're waiting for you."

Makhi nodded and rushed past Grandmother to go downstairs.

CHAPTER FOUR

The Visit

I grew somewhat apprehensive as we rode toward the uncles' house, but I wasn't sure why. It had been nearly a month since I'd seen Makhi. Visiting typically stirred excitement within me. I didn't understand these new feelings.

"Are you quite alright?" Mother squeezed my knee from the front seat.

Startled, I gasped. I'd been so lost in thought that I didn't see her turn around and touch me. Wide-eyed, I stared at Mother. "Y-Yes," I stumbled. "I'm okay. I was just thinking."

"Father called your name three times. Don't you think you should answer him?" Mother reprimanded softly.

I looked apologetically at Father's eyes in the rearview mirror. "I'm so—"

"Don't worry, Beloved. What's wrong?" I shrugged. I truly didn't know.

"Hanen!" Mother's tone was sharp this time. "Don't be rude to your father!"

Father swallowed hard. "Um… I'm sure she didn't mean anything by it. Did you, Hanen?"

I shook my head, "No, Father. I didn't."

"See there. All our girls are golden." Father smiled in the rearview mirror and sighed.

The van slowed, turned into the uncles' driveway, and parked in front of their two-car garage next to Uncle Arif's old, blue jeep.

"Were they watching for us?" Mother laughed.

Confused, I looked up from my book. Two of my uncles were bounding down the patio steps toward us with big smiles on their faces.

"Hello there!" Uncle Arif greeted each of us with a hug as we clamored out of the van. Then, he put his hands in his pockets and watched us unload, seeming to be at a loss.

"Are you going to invite us in or leave us sitting in the heat?"

"Oh! Right!" Uncle Arif chuckled. "Let me help you with your bags." Walking around to Mother's side of the van, he helped her with her door before going to the back and retrieving our suitcase and Mother's toiletry bag.

After we were all inside, Grandmother Fatima hugged everyone. Then she shooed my sisters and me outside to play, "There's not enough room in this tiny house for everyone. And there's already too much commotion. Go play!"

"Here, Shameera," Grandmother handed her a large silver colander. "There are a few small date palms on the southwest edge of the property. Be a dear and collect some."

The way Mother looked at Grandmother Fatima just then was one of both disbelief and severe disapproval, "I don't—"

Grandmother Fatima held up her hand to silence Mother. Her mouth fell open, and her incredulous look transformed into a glare. "The dates are ripe," Grandma continued in a calm tone. Then she looked at Mother and smiled as sweetly as she could, "Makhi will go with you."

Mother's composure relaxed slightly, but I could tell she was still ticked off.

Grandmother Fatima looked at Makhi, "Have them back in time to wash for dinner."

Makhi looked from Grandmother Fatima to Mother and back again. He didn't look like he knew *what* to do or *whose* side he should take.

"Makhi?" Grandmother Fatima was more forceful this time. Her voice always carried an air of authority, but this went a step further. She almost growled, demanding respect and immediate action.

Makhi was startled, "On it!" He grabbed Bayza's and my hands and started for the door, Shameera close on his heels.

***

"The palm is Iraq's national symbol," Makhi told us. "We used to have over 30 million palm trees in our country. They were dying out due to conflict and blight. Some people across Iraq chose to plant new trees—a few here and there. It added up to many newly planted palm trees."

I smiled widely. *Makhi is so smart!*

"Wow!" said Shameera in awe, "How do you know so much?" "You learn a lot in high school, Squirt," he laughed as he tussled Shameera's hair.

Makhi looked my way and winked. I beamed and sighed a special sigh. He didn't treat *me* that way—like a little girl. He treated *me* like his equal, like the woman I'd one day grow up to be. It made me feel special inside, like I was special to Makhi. It was almost magical.

"Alright, ladies, I think we have enough dates."

I looked down at the colander in my hands. "It's overflowing," I giggled, holding it up for all to see.

Makhi nodded. "Do you remember the way home, Beloved?"

I tilted my head a bit and squinted as I plotted each landmark on the trail we had taken. "Yes," I said confidently. "I think so?" I added a little less so as my eyebrows rose.

"Alright!" He hoisted Bayza on his shoulders. "Lead the way, trusty guide." The way his eyes sparkled gave me confidence and energy.

Nodding, I turned and led us toward the uncles' house.

***

As we walked into the house, the scent of fresh-baked samoon and Grandmother Fatima's famous soup teased our noses. My stomach growled loudly, making us all laugh.

Mother rushed around the corner, "Well, it's about time! I've been worried sick! Where have you been?"

"Hello, Lana." Makhi kissed her on the cheek. "Here are your dates!"

Mother glared at Makhi. "I didn't want the dates. Grandmother Fatima did, and don't try to get out of this! You were to be home half an hour ago!"

"It's Hanen's fault!" blurted out Shameera. "She took a left at the double cactus instead of a right. I told her we should go right, but she didn't listen!"

I folded my hands in front of me and hung my head. "I—"

"Don't blame her," started Makhi. "It was every bit my—"

"I don't care whose fault it was, "interrupted Mother. "You were late. That's that. Now get washed up for dinner." With that, she turned on her heel and returned to where she had come from.

We all looked at each other, wondering how we had gotten out of a lashing. Then Makhi started to laugh.

"Shh! Don't laugh, Makhi. She'll come back!" Shameera whispered.

He quickly quieted, and we all headed toward the bathroom, but it wasn't long before we were following our noses toward the dining room.

Makhi pasted on one of his best smiles, "Sorry we're late, but we brought the *best* fresh dates!" He paused and sniffed the air. "Mmm! Is that Samoon?" He reached for a roll and bit into it. He half closed his eyes, making a show of savoring the bread while his brothers glowered at him.

"Late and disrespectful as usual, I see, "Ibrahim glared at him.

Makhi turned to Ibrahim and bowed with exaggerated humility. "My lord Ibrahim, please forgive your unworthy servant."

Ibrahim's scowl deepened. "You're far too old to behave like such a child, Makhi. Your mother and sister have slaved over this meal, and you arrive late, smelling of dust and sweat."

"Brother, are you suggesting I should not have gone and spent time with my lovely nieces?"

I giggled, and Makhi turned and winked at me. Ibrahim reddened and opened his mouth to fire back, but Grandmother Fatima spread her hands and looked up. "In the name of God, the merciful, Allah grant us grace." Opening her eyes, she lowered her hands and sat gracefully at the table with a smile on her face.

Everyone respectfully turned to their food. Ibrahim, Elham, and Shameera's sour expressions grew more contented as their bellies filled. After a few spoonfuls, even Mother mellowed.

I loved Grandmother Fatima's cooking, and her special soup is my favorite of all her recipes. I must have eaten almost three bowls and half a samoon before I finally sat back and rubbed my belly, admitting defeat.

Suddenly, Makhi pushed away from the table, patted his stomach, and loudly burped. The adults frowned, but it made Bayza and me giggle. Even Shameera smiled, though she tried to hide it behind her napkin.

"Well, that was the best soup I've had in a very long while." He stood up and stretched toward the ceiling, "My compliments to the chef. I think I'll go wash. When I'm clean, I think I'll go on a bike ride. Hanen, would you like to join me?"

"Oh, yes, please!" I bounced in my seat excitedly, "Please, may I? Please?"

"Me too?" Bayza asked.

"When you're a little older, precious," Makhi said. "Nighttime bike rides are only for grownups."

"Neen's not!" Bayza crossed her arms and stuck out her lip.

"Yeah!" Shameera protested, wrinkling her brow like Father does so often. "Hanen's not a grown-up!"

"She's not?" Makhi said incredulously. I flushed as he looked me up and down appraisingly. "She looks pretty grown up to me." He stepped closer and looked me up and down again, a look of concentration on his face. "Are you sure about that, Shameera?"

A grin spread across my face, and I puffed out my chest. I really liked it when Makhi called me a grown-up. It made me feel even more important!

"She can't go out this late," Shameera said. "Mother, tell Makhi he can't take Hanen out."

I frowned at my big sister. *Why does Shameera have to ruin everything?*

"Shameera's right. You're too young—"

"Lana, I think a short bike ride might be just what the girl needs," Grandmother Fatima smiled conspiratorially. "What do you think, Ayad?"

Father swallowed hard and set his cup of tea down on the table. Shaking his head, "I'm afraid not. I must stand by her mother in this."

I let my gaze trace slowly toward grandmother. Her mouth fell open slightly. Then she pursed her lips and submissively nodded her head. "Very well."

Makhi cleared his throat, "May I propose we pull the play station out?"

I squealed as I jumped up from my chair, nearly toppling it backward, and ran to Makhi, wrapping him in a bear hug. He lifted me off the ground and squeezed me close for a long moment. Then he lowered me back to the ground.

CHAPTER FIVE

Beginning of the Darkness

I peered around in the large living room in the almost complete darkness. Shameera, Bayza, and I were the first three sleeping, but the rest of the family had chosen spots around us to lay their mats and bedded down for the night not long after we did.

The only sounds I could hear were the crickets chirping and an owl calling off in the distance. There was cool air blowing on my face from somewhere. *Perhaps from the vent under the window?*

Suddenly, something moved off to my right. I jumped and gasped. *It's my imagination.* I tightly closed my eyes and reminded myself, *It's just my imagination.* But when I opened them, a tall, lone figure was crouched beside me. A chill passed down my spine. I opened my mouth to shriek, but a hand covered my mouth and silenced me.

"Hanen!" came a gentle but harried whisper. "It's just me, Makhi! It's okay!" There was a pause. I think Makhi was trying to see my face in the darkness, just as I was trying to see his. "Are you okay?"

I nodded my head.

"Good. I'm going to let go of your mouth. We need to keep quiet now. We don't want to wake the others and make anyone angry."

When he took his hand off my mouth, I gasped as quietly as I could for air. I don't think he realized he was half covering my nose, restricting my airway.

"I have something I want to show you." Makhi took my hand and led me toward the dining room door.

I paused, "But shouldn't we tell Mother if we're going somewhere?"

"Oh! Don't worry. She knows that you're safe with me. Besides, you turn six in a few days! You're big enough to go on adventures with Makhi, aren't you?"

"Yeah. I guess so, but I—" "Good then. It's settled!

I tried to smile, but I swallowed around the lump in my throat instead. Was it right to go somewhere without telling Mother? I didn't know. *But Makhi says it's okay. And he wouldn't lie. So, it must be okay. Right?* I felt my anxiety begin to melt away. *Surely Makhi would never steer me wrong. Not Makhi.*

I did smile, then. Spending time alone with Makhi was always special, but this new adventure was a secret adventure! That made it almost magical! It was for me and me alone. No one else.

"Okay, Hanen. We have to be very careful now." I could feel his face next to mine. "We must watch where we step and be very, very quiet. Otherwise, our secret adventure will be ruined."

Nodding, I held my breath and peered harder into the darkness. I tried to walk exactly where Makhi walked, step for step. But I don't think I could have bumped into anyone since Makhi held my hand so tightly.

It was little things like that which made Uncle Makhi my favorite. He treated me like I was precious to him and deserved the attention he gave me. I mattered to Makhi. To Makhi, I was old enough to share secrets with. Adults don't share secrets with children. They share secrets in hushed tones, and when the children come close, they stop talking altogether. But Makhi was sharing a secret with *me*! He was treating *me* like an adult! Because I was important to him!

We reached the dining room doorway. Makhi's breathing quickened. *Are we going on another nighttime bike ride? Or to the tarma to look at the stars?* But then, Makhi led me to the left hallway, which led to the back of the house. I looked at him questioningly but followed. We stopped in front of the washroom, and he gently pushed the white paneled door open. Leading me inside, he shut and locked the door after us.

"Makhi?"

He stared at me and raised his eyebrows. I took that as his permission to proceed with my question.

"Why are we in here?" I waved my hand toward the toilet and tub. I knew everything there was to know about the washroom. What could he possibly show me in there?

"Hush now." My eyes grew wide, and I jolted to attention. Something was wrong. The tone of his voice was different than I'd ever heard it before. It was sharper and more urgent.

"What's the matter, Uncle Makhi?" I almost forgot to whisper.

Makhi shook his head and ran his hand through his hair. "Nothing's wrong. I just don't want anyone else to wake up and interrupt our special time together." His voice sounded somewhat normal now.

It was cheerful, but I could still hear his desperation under the cheerfulness. Surely there was something wrong. He used the same tone my parents used when Bayza, Shameera, or I accidentally walked in on them discussing a serious matter. They used the tone to reassure us so we wouldn't be worried about whatever we walked in on. Still, it always made me more nervous because I knew Mother and Father were worried, and I didn't know why. But prying into it never got me answers, and I didn't figure it would with Makhi either. But the fear remained, squeezing my chest like an invisible hand.

Makhi crouched next to me. The nightlight over the sink cast an eerie glow over him. I could see he was smiling, but I couldn't tell if it was a real or fake smile that adults wore when telling kids not to worry.

"We're going to play a different kind of game, Hanen." His voice was back to normal. No more desperation or urgency that had worried me a moment before. I relaxed and returned his smile. "It's going to be really fun, but you can't tell anyone about it, okay?"

I nodded.

"They won't understand it, and anyway, this is just special for you and me. No one else, okay?"

"Okay. I won't tell."

I crossed my arms over my stomach, hugging myself. It bothered me that he was worried about me talking.

"Good. Now close your eyes. I'm going to show you something really fun!"

Excitedly, I squeezed my eyes shut and waited. The faucet was dripping again. *What's that?* Makhi's breathing sounded strange again.

It sounded fast and ragged like he'd been running for a long time. I felt the warmth of his body as he leaned closer to me, and I could feel his breath on my face. I could smell it too. It wasn't bad, a little sour from the laban we had after dinner, but not terrible. Nonetheless, I suddenly felt sick to my stomach. I popped open my eyes and instinctively pulled my face away from Makhi's breath.

"There's nothing to be afraid of," he whispered. Placing his hand behind my head, he leaned in again. I tried to pull away again, but I couldn't! He held me so tightly that I couldn't move my head even an inch. His lips closed over mine. He was trying to kiss me! But it wasn't the normal kiss like the way Grandmother or Mother gave kisses. No! This was far different! He was sucking my lips and licking them. His mouth was open, and his breath—*Oh! His breath!* It assaulted me, filling my nose, airways, and lungs. A shiver of disgust passed down my spine.

Why is he doing this? It felt so wrong. I tried turning my head away, but he was too strong. He kept sliding his gross, slimy tongue over my lips as I kept them clamped tightly shut. It reminded me of a snail. Another shiver.

Makhi pulled away, and I gasped for air. *Finally!* Relief washed over me. I did *not* like this game. It was *not* fun at all. Perhaps if I told Makhi, we could go back to bed and do something different in the morning?

But Makhi wasn't done. "Open your mouth." his whisper was ragged.

I stood staring at him in disbelief. *Open my mouth? Why?* I was suddenly terrified. What was he going to do? I shook my head.

"Open your mouth." His voice was a little louder, more demanding, and insistent. "Please," he added, deliberately softening his tone once more.

Leaning in, he began kissing me again. Using his right hand, the hand that wasn't holding my head, he pinched my jaw, forcing my lips apart. His movements suddenly grew more urgent. He gripped my head so tightly that it hurt me. His breathing was hard and ragged again.

I desperately wanted to push him away, to tell him to stop. I didn't like this game! I just wanted to go back to bed. But I couldn't move. I was frozen, rooted to the spot where I stood, as though I were glued down. And as I stood there, unable to do anything but accept my fate, he continued kissing me.

Once more, he pulled away, and I gasped for clean air. *Is this a trick? Is he going to start back again? Or do something worse?* I stared at him, my eyes wide open, begging for answers but not wanting to know what they were. He released my head and stood up.

I stood silently before him, unable to meet his eyes. I wanted to tell him what was on my mind—that I didn't like that game and please not to do it again. I wanted to ask him why. But I couldn't form the words, so I just stood there staring at the marble floors. For the first time I could remember, I felt uncomfortable around Uncle Makhi. I just wanted him to leave, to go back to bed so I could wash his taste out of my mouth. And this feeling of wanting him to get away from me was almost as frightening as what had happened. *I love Makhi. Don't I?*

"Okay, Hanen. I'm going to bed." He walked to the door and paused. "Don't tell anyone. Promise?"

I nodded, but I still didn't say anything. I stared at the floor once more. I heard Makhi open and shut the door and listened as he walked down the hallway to the living room. As soon as I could no longer hear his footsteps, I raced to the sink and began to spit and gag. I could still feel his nasty tongue sliding around my mouth. My skin still felt like it was crawling.

I turned on the cold water. Scooping it into my mouth, I swished and spat, but the awful taste was difficult to wash away. I grabbed my toothbrush from the holder so forcefully that I almost pulled the whole thing off the wall! Squirting a large amount of toothpaste on my toothbrush, I began brushing vigorously. Thirty seconds. Forty. Fifty. A minute.

I filled my toothbrush again with paste and continued brushing. I brushed my gums, my tongue, and the roof of my mouth. My arm grew tired, and I switched to the other before the minty flavor of the Crest finally replaced Makhi's laban-soured breath.

Suddenly, I froze! I thought I heard a footfall. I held my breath and listened carefully. *The light!* I tiptoed as quickly and quietly as I could to the door and flipped off the switch. I didn't want whoever to see the light under the door. I waited with bated breath, but I never heard another thing. Realizing it was my imagination; I decided not to flip the light back on. After all, I had been making so much noise, it was a wonder that Mother or Grandmother Fatima hadn't come investigating! Slowly opening the door, I peeked into the hallway, but nobody was there.

I timidly started down the hallway after softly closing the door behind me. An unusual brightness drew me to the window over the sink in the kitchen. *Is the morning coming already? How long were we in the bathroom?!* I didn't even need to stand on my tiptoes to see the moon was high in the sky and as big as life itself. Only, it wasn't the regular moon. It was red, like an evil red eye, glowing in the sky. But maybe it wasn't evil. I had always imagined that the moon was my friend. But perhaps it was angry with me because I couldn't stop Makhi, even though I wanted to. Perhaps the moon didn't know I couldn't move. Maybe its eye was red from anger, anger at me.

A strong foreboding and heavy sadness overtook my anxiety as I slowly turned from the window and tiptoed to the living room door. I held my breath and peeked around the corner, allowing my eyes to adjust to the further darkness of the room. *Thank Allah!* All my family were still sleeping soundly. And Makhi was sleeping on the far left of the living room, opposite me, facing the wall. Maybe he wouldn't hear me go to my mat, either.

After avoiding everyone as I tiptoed through the living room, I snuggled into my blankets, but try as I might, sleep eluded me. I merely lay there staring at the ceiling, remembering what had happened, yet trying to forget.

CHAPTER SIX

Deep Pain

Present Day, Our Apartment

I woke up with the events of the evening before fresh on my mind. *I can't believe I reacted that way! And to my own husband!* Fresh tears pressed on the backs of my eyes, and I sighed loudly. At least I felt much better this morning.

I felt Akmal shift in bed beside me. *Sorry!* I turned to look just in time to see him roll up on one elbow. Reaching out, he tenderly brushed my hair behind my ear, "How are you feeling, *Habibti*?"

I held my breath, waiting for the same feelings as last night. But they didn't come. I breathed a sigh of relief. I smiled and covered his hand with mine, hugging it to my face. "I'm feeling much better now, thanks to you." after getting ready to do my duty as a wife. In my head I am not forced to do that when I am not okay with it. If I tell Akmal, but I feel bad because he is the best man who treatz me like a prince. He deserves to enjoy his wife. And that is what matters... the feeling of this is not my body wasn't mine to own, it belongs to another.

Then, I remembered the plans he had for last night. I remembered the candles behind the picture frame. "I'm so sorry, Akmal," I looked deep into his brown eyes, begging forgiveness, "for ruining last night."

"Hey," Akmal stroked my chin with his thumb. "Stop that. No night is ruined with you, *Habibti*. I'm just glad you're feeling better!"

***

After Akmal left for work, I grabbed the phone and dialed Sama's number. It was early afternoon in Baghdad. Hopefully, she would be home and answer the phone. I desperately needed to speak to someone. I couldn't carry this on my own anymore.

I decided to risk her judgment and disgust if I could unburden my soul.

The phone rang once, twice, four times, and my heart sank into my stomach. I didn't think I could work up the courage to do this again. Just as I was about to hang up, Sama answered breathlessly.

"Hana, is that you?" She asked.

"Yes, Sama, it's me. You sound out of breath. Did you just run a marathon?" I tried to joke.

"As if," she shot back at me, "No, I was just out on the roof trying to catch a breeze to cool down."

"That makes sense," I mumbled, the nerves making it hard to think of anything else to say.

"Hanen, are you okay? You don't sound like yourself." she asked, the worry evident in her voice.

I took a deep breath, trying to calm my racing heart and roiling stomach. "No, Sama. I'm not alright. I haven't been alright in a long time."

"Hana, what's going on? You're worrying me! Are things bad with Akmal?" she demanded.

"No, no. Akmal is as sweet as ever. He is a good man, much too good for me." I added quietly.

"That's crazy talk, Hana. You deserve all the beautiful, sparkly, and good things in life. Akmal is lucky to have you as a wife!" She added emphatically.

"He deserves so much better. You just don't know the truth about me. I came to him dirty and sullied. I've been unclean since I was six years old." I sobbed, pushing the words out between big gulps of air.

"Hanen, I need you to tell me what you are talking about right now! You are saying crazy things, and I'm really worried about you. I haven't seen you cry since you fell out of the date tree and sprained your ankle when you were nine years old! I've known you most of our lives. Please tell me what is going on," she implored me.

"Do you remember my Uncle Makhi?" I asked between sobs.

"I remember Makhi. You two always seemed really close. Did something happen to Makhi? Did he die?" Sama grasped at straws in her attempt to figure out what was going on with me.

"I think he's fine. I haven't talked to him in a long time. This has to do with things that happened a long time ago." I paused, gathering the courage to continue. "One night, when I was six years old, Makhi woke me up and brought me to the washroom. That night he kissed me; like a real adult kiss, kissed me. Things only got worse from there. He kept it up until I was sixteen." I could barely speak; I was sobbing so hard. It was like 19 years of trauma, and pain had been held back by a dam that had burst. I was being washed away in a tidal wave of unbearable pain. "I'll understand if you never want to talk to me again.

I know I'm not who you thought. I'm so full of sin and shame." I whispered the last sentence. It hurt to admit it aloud.

"Hana, oh Hana," Sama was sobbing on the other side of the phone, "Hana, I am so sorry that happened to you. I'm sorry I didn't see it and didn't help you. You're right. You aren't who I thought you were. You are stronger and more beautiful. You are not dirty or sinful. Makhi is the sinner! I want to claw his eyes out for what he did to you! Why did you never tell me? I can't even hug you right now! I hate that I can't hug and look you in your eyes. I want you to see how much I love you."

I didn't think it was possible to cry any harder, but I was wrong. The tears continued unabashed, but they felt different. Instead of tears of shame, these felt like healing tears.

"I didn't know how to tell anyone. I thought something was wrong with me, that it was my fault." I explained.

"You did NOTHING wrong. Makhi was an adult, a disgusting pedophile. You were an innocent six-year-old child. I understand you couldn't say anything, but I wish I could have helped you." Sama paused and then continued, "Does Akmal know?"

"No one knows, except you," I told her.

"You've never told anyone? Until today? You've carried this burden all alone all these years? Oh, my dear friend, I am so sorry for all you've been through! But you are no longer alone. I will help you. You know you need to tell Akmal, right?" She asked the one question I hoped that she wouldn't.

"I can't tell him! He calls me his "pure Hanen." How can I tell him I haven't been pure since I was six? He could leave me!"

"Akmal loves you more than life itself. I can almost promise he will not blame you for what was done to you. He needs to know so he can understand and help you. He's your husband. Would you judge him if this happened to him as a child?" Sama asked me.

"Of course not! I would want to kill whoever hurt him, but I would never blame him!" I said emphatically.

"Then trust that he will not blame you either."

"I just can't tell him yet. But I will try." I tried to assure her.

"If you can't talk to Akmal yet, at least promise me that you will find a therapist and start going to therapy. You need someone to help you process all of this. I will talk to you any time, but I am half a globe away. You need someone on the same continent, preferably in your town."

"I will look for a therapist," I promised.

After a few moments longer, we hung up. I then Googled "therapist near me." I scrolled through several names. I wasn't comfortable talking to a male therapist, so I eliminated them from the possibilities. Still, there were so many names. How was I supposed to make a choice? I knew nothing about any of them. I continued scanning down the list. Suddenly, a face jumped out at me. Dr. Allison Peters. The bio under her picture and contact info said she specialized in PTSD and early childhood trauma. She had a kind face. My gut told me to call her. I sent Allah a quick prayer for wisdom and dialed the phone.

Ten minutes later, my first therapy session was scheduled for a week from that day.

***

A week later, I was still reflecting on the events of that morning. *Akmal is so kind to me.* I meticulously arranged the sautéed scallops and roasted vegetables on the blue China plates, a birthday gift from Sama, my best friend. She sent them from Iraq, so she had to ship them two months earlier for them to arrive on time.

When I called Iraq to thank Sama for the beautiful plates, her first question was, "Did they make it in one piece?" She had asked it so slowly and with so much guilt that I hated to tell her one of the plates was broken, but I couldn't lie.

"I'm so sorry, Hanen! I'll call customer service and make it right!"

"Oh! Honey! Don't worry about it! It's perfectly fine. Besides, seven is the perfect amount. You know that's my favorite number. I've always held that it's Allah's favorite digit too!"

"I still don't get that, Hanen. You know that Allah's favorite number is 786."

"Yes, but the first digit of that is?" "Seven…"

"And there are seven ayat in al-Fatiha, the first surat in the Quran. Pilgrims perform seven walks during both Umrah and Hajj. Pilgrims going to Mecca make seven circumambulations around the Kaaba. Our babies are named on the seventh day. There are seven Earths and seven Heavens. And the list goes on!" I smiled at the silence on the other end of the phone. I could imagine Sama's mouth hanging open like it always did when I spouted things she had no idea I knew. "Oh! And there are seven enunciators of divine revelation!"

"Are you through?" Sama spoke with awe after a short silence. "Yes." I positively glowed.

"Okay. You proved your point. I won't worry about the eighth plate."

"Thank you very much. Glad to be of help." I didn't tell her I had called customer service about the plate, trying to get it replaced. They were quite unhelpful, though. They just kept referring to all the bombs being dropped during the time it took to ship the package. That may be why it took two months for me to receive my package, but that's not why a plate was broken. Their reasoning was null and void.

"Anyway," Sama had continued. "I hope things have been well there. Did you talk to Akmal? Have you scheduled therapy?"

"Things are going fine. No, I haven't told him yet. And yes, I did schedule the appointment."

"I'm so glad you are going." Sama seemed relieved. "I've been so worried about you."

"Do you like charcoal with your side of scallops, or did you just forget about them?" Allisa's question jarred me from reverie and back to the present.

"Oh no!" I quickly poured the burnt scallops from the pan, dumping them on the plate. My shoulders slumped forward as I released a deep sigh. *I ruined dinner.* I felt my face flush and hot tears pressed against the backs of my eyelids. *I can't do anything right.* Dropping the pan on the stove, I slumped in a chair and buried my face in my hands.

Allisa rushed over and threw her arms around me. "Honey! I'm so sorry! I was just teasing. Honest!" She stooped down in front of me and carefully took my hands in hers so she could look into my face. "They're not burnt. They'll be okay! It's nothing a little citrus and ginger sauce can't cure." She tilted her head and smiled, and I nodded, though it was almost imperceptible.

I took a shaky breath. I still wasn't crying, but my eyes were swimming with tears. "It's not that. I just wanted tonight to be perfect—for Akmal. After last week… After I ruined everything… I don't know." I dropped my eyes and watched as I interlaced my fingers. "I just wanted to do something special for him."

"After last week? Honey! You got food poisoning. That's not your fault. You couldn't do anything about that."

I pursed my lips and shook my head. *But it wasn't food poisoning, and it was my fault.* A single tear fell from my eye.

Allisa wiped the tear from my cheek with the back of her fingers. "Sweetie? What's wrong?" Her brow wrinkled in thought. "This isn't just about last week, is it?"

My breath caught in my throat, and my muscles tensed. *I can't tell her.* I didn't know *what* to tell her.

The sound of running sneakers, backpacks tossed on the entryway bench, and excited voices interrupted us. Relief flooded over me as I shifted in my chair. *Thank You, Allah!*

"Saved by the bell," teased Allisa as she rolled her eyes and stood up. "Looks like your little monsters rescued you once more."

I jumped to my feet. I needed some space before Allisa could ask any more questions. I suddenly felt dizzy but took a deep breath to steady myself. "I'll get them an afterschool snack."

"No. No!" Allisa called over her shoulder as she rushed off toward the entryway. "You worry about your scallops." She paused in the hallway. "I wouldn't want you to overcook the sauce by thirty seconds and collapse into a nervous wreck on the kitchen floor," she grinned slyly.

I couldn't help but smile as I thanked her. But my smile disappeared when she started down the hall. I felt like such a hypocrite. *If she knew—*

I spooned some sauce on a teaspoon and put it to my lips. *Perfect.* As I spooned some over the scallops, a smile returned to my lips, and my spirits lightened somewhat. Allisa had been right. The sauce lent a nice shine to the scallops, giving them an appealing, gently burnished look. *Perhaps, Akmal will still like them.*

"Click," the front door opening greeted my ears, but even sweeter were the strains of music from my husband humming. I smiled. *He's happy.*

Grabbing the plates from the counter, I rushed to set them in their places on the dining room table. Then I lit the two candle sticks in the centerpiece.

I was still pouring the sparkling water into Akmal's glass when he laced his arms around my waist from the back and kissed my neck. "Good evening, my love."

My heart jumped into my throat, but I managed not to react as I set the carafe down.

He turned me around and stared deep into my eyes, "What's the occasion?" The light in his eyes matched his bright smile. I couldn't help but return it.

"Nothing, Amiri. I just wanted to show you how much I adore you."

He gently ran the back of his hand down my cheek before kissing me tenderly. "Maybe I can return the favor later."

I giggled, but the suggestion of sex brought a flood of negative feelings. I hoped the emotion didn't reach my eyes. *That's the way to ruin the—*

Footsteps sounded behind me on the ceramic tile as Allisa, Hamsa, and Hamid rounded the corner into the kitchen. "Can we have Oreos for our snack," Hamid asked. His sweet tooth was legendary. Akmal grinned and grabbed the box of cookies before I could object. Hamid gave Akmal a high five and snagged a couple of cookies from the box. Hamsa poured herself a glass of grape juice and took two cookies.

"I'm going to head on toward home, then," she nodded to me. "I think I've bothered the two of you enough."

"Oh, you're never a bother!" Akmal smiled politely. "Why don't you stay for dinner?"

Allisa laughed, "I don't know, Akmal. If I stay, I might fall in love with Hanen's cooking and steal her from you." She winked at me.

"In that case, out of my house!" Akmal pointed toward the door playfully. "She's mine! I saw her first!"

"That means nothing!" Allisa called over her shoulder as she gathered her pocketbook and keys from the baker's rack in the corner. "Hanen, honey, I'll call you tomorrow, okay?"

After their snack, the children ran off to do their homework and then played with their friends for an hour as I finished dinner.

When everything was perfect, I called my family to the table for dinner. Once they were seated, I sat across from Akmal.

He looked up and smiled lovingly when he noticed I had sat down.

"Let us ask Allah's blessing and eat this wonderful meal you prepared!"

I smiled sheepishly. *I sure hope he likes it!* I cut a small piece of scallop and timidly took my first bite. The sauce had soaked into the meat, leaving it juicy, tangy, and just a hint of savory. I tasted a carrot and onions together. *Perfect!* The roasted vegetables were a perfect complement. They mellowed the tartness of the sauce without completely obscuring it. *I did it! The perfect dinner!*

"Hanen! Where did you get this recipe?" Akmal put another bite of scallop in his mouth and closed his eyes. "It's *so* good it just explodes on your tongue!"

"Oh! This? I just made it up." I winced at the lie as my heart jumped in my chest. Surely, he'd never learn I'd found it online. *No man wants a wife who has to look up how to make such a simple dinner.*

"Look at you!" Akmal sat back in his chair and grinned from ear to ear. "So full of surprises. I find something new to love about you every day."

I felt the heat rise in my cheeks and up my neck. I hoped my husband took it for a blush rather than the embarrassment it was. I tried to focus on the pride I should feel from the praise rather than the guilt from knowing the praise was undeserved.

Hamid shoveled food into his mouth so fast it was amazing he could taste anything. "Slow down, Hamid. The scallops will not get up and run away," I laughed.

"Adnan and Faisal are waiting for me," he explained, barely breathing between bites.

"Hamid, your mother spent a lot of time cooking us this beautiful meal. Respect her work and slow down. If you take ten extra minutes to eat and digest your food, your friends will still be waiting to play Fortnight with you." Akmal gave him a look that allowed for no arguments.

"Yes, Father." Hamid sighed and looked at his plate.

"Now tell your mother thank you for dinner, and then tell us about your day." Akmal smiled at him encouragingly.

I loved these moments with our family, sitting around the table, sharing about our days. The children were growing so fast. Hamsa was already twelve, almost a teenager! And Hamid wasn't far behind her at ten. How is it possible that time has flown by so fast? It seemed like I was a brand-new bride arriving in this country only yesterday.

I listened as Hamid told us about running drills at football, err, soccer practice. Then Hamsa told us about the new girl in her biology class. We all laughed at Hamid's eye roll when Hamsa mentioned that the girl had an older brother.

"Mom, tell him not to tease me." Hamsa pleaded.

"Hamid, don't tease your sister." Hoping to avoid an argument, I quickly changed the subject. "How was work?" I asked Akmal.

Akmal shrugged. "The same. Retail work isn't exactly the most glamorous job in the world."

"Can I get up and play on the Xbox now?" Hamid interjected.

"Finish eating and take out the trash. Then you may play with them. Hamsa, it is your turn to do the dishes." With that, they were silently eating, hurrying to finish and do their own things. We wouldn't have them home with us for too many more years, I thought sadly.

I quietly stood and shuffled toward Akmal, wanting to make him feel better. I could tell he was a bit discouraged with his job. My feet felt heavy. I breathed deeply, trying to quiet my anxiety and relax my body. I swayed my hips enticingly as I walked behind him and leaned over, allowing my arms to slide down his chest. "My poor, hardworking man," I crooned. "Hurry up and finish your dinner so I can make it all better."

Akmal tilted his head back and stared at me with big eyes, "What's gotten into you?"

What did I do? "You don't like it?" I teased with a pouty voice.

He grinned and put his free hand over mine. "I love it! I'm unsure what I did to put you in such a great mood."

I kissed his forehead, "I'm your wife. It's my job to keep you happy."

"Gross!" Hamid rolled his eyes. At ten, he thought any kind of affection was "gross."

Hamsa laughed at his reaction. She thought of herself as quite grown up at twelve.

I looked at Hamid, sighed loudly, feigning disappointment, and walked toward my son, allowing my hands to slide from Akmal's shoulders. I could never tell him the truth—I was relieved to stop touching him.

"Hamid, if you are done with dinner, remember to take out the garbage, and then you can play with your friends for another thirty minutes." I reminded him.

"I'm done eating too. Can I watch TV?" Hamsa asked.

I looked at her plate and quickly gauged how much she had eaten. It looked like she had eaten almost half. That was good. "Yes, after you finish loading the dishwasher. Dad and I will finish dinner and join you in watching TV."

We finished dinner, talking and laughing like we used to when we first married. I continued flirting with Akmal. Though the thought of sex still made my flesh crawl, I pushed the feelings down by focusing on my husband's excitement at the thought of being with me.

I looked at my husband. He had such a beautiful heart. He deserved a wife who enjoyed touching him, not a broken girl who hated to be kissed. *I* **will** *be that good wife tonight. I don't care how it makes me feel.*

It suddenly struck me that I never remembered Mother making the same effort for Father. I knew they loved each other and were intimate—at least occasionally. Still, I never saw Mother go out of her way to please Father. I was sure it was something she didn't enjoy, that it was something she viewed as an obligation. Of course, we never talked about any of this, but I noticed things. *I felt the same way about my night with Makhi and—*

I suddenly gasped and jumped at the thought. Akmal's eyes grew wide in alarm. "Are you alright?"

"I… I'm okay," I stumbled. "I just bit my tongue."

"Okay…" He seemed to relax a little but continued watching me intently. *He knows it's a lie.*

I quickly shoveled my last bite into my mouth and swallowed. "I'm fine." I smiled compellingly, "Let's go watch TV with Hamsa until we can have some time alone together." I attempted to give him a coy smile.

Akmal's breathing sped up, and his pupils dilated as he swallowed with nervous anticipation. *Focus on that, Hanen. Your husband is happy. That's what counts. It's about him. Not… anything else.*

Later that night, after the children were in their rooms, I took a deep breath and tried to slow my breathing. *Too fast.* As I walked toward my bedroom, my heart pounded. My hands were clammy, and the back of my neck felt cold. I tried to swallow, but my mouth was so dry that there was no saliva. *Why am I so nervous? He's my husband!* We'd made love so many times! Why was I so suddenly repulsed by the thought? Why were these childhood memories haunting me again after all these years?

I stood in front of the mirror. I was petite, but I also knew I was very attractive. At least Akmal said so. And that's what mattered. He often told me how privileged he felt that I belonged to him, and he said it was a gift he thanked Allah for every day.

I always agreed with him and said how thankful I was that I had saved myself for him. It killed me to lie to him like that. He called me his pure Hanen. *If he knew I was so soiled when he met me… If he knew now…*

I wasn't pure. I was far from pure. *Dirty. Soiled. Used. That's what I am. Long ago.* I felt the tears pressing on the backs of my eyes. From my youth, I'd been abused and used as a wife by a man who had no business touching me. I was supposed to belong only to my husband, but my innocence was stolen from me long before he met me.

Hearing Akmal's footsteps on the stairs, my anxiety grew, my heart began to race, and I smiled as big as I could as he stepped in the door smiling. "You are so beautiful, *Habibti*," he half whispered.

***

I lay there feeling like I'd done something wrong or been wronged. But I reminded myself that this was far from the truth. *My body belongs to my husband. I love him, and he loves me. He didn't steal anything.* But no matter how much I told myself the truth, these lies permeated my heart and soul.

Finally, Akmal's breathing had slowed, and I knew he was asleep, but I found a way to go to the other room.

I did start weeping then. I covered my mouth with my free hand, so I wouldn't wake Akmal. All I could think of was Makhi. His hot breath on me. I hated him. Hated that he had ruined me. I hated myself for being ruined. I hated Akmal for lying with me and hated myself even more for hating him just because he was enjoying the pleasures Allah awarded him.

Did Makhi know he made me feel this way? He knew I hadn't enjoyed what he did to me. I'd made that crystal clear when I finally gathered the courage to demand that he leave me alone. *Finally. Why didn't I do it sooner? Did he ever think about the pain he was causing? The future pain? I wonder if he knew I wouldn't be able to enjoy my own husband because of him. Because of his abuse…*

I tried to fight the thoughts, drive them out of my head, and chase them away. But they kept tormenting me. I had been holding them back all evening, and I was exhausted. Now, I could only weep while the memories ravaged me, repeatedly traumatizing me as I lay next to my husband.

*****

Office of Dr. Allison Peters, Alberta, Canada

I sat on a dark brown leather sofa, nervously picking at invisible lint on my slacks. Dr. Peters sat next to me in an overstuffed blue chair. I would guess she was in her forties. She had mid-length blonde hair and green eyes behind a pair of bright pink glasses. She was slightly overweight and had a pretty smile. I silently sat, waiting for her to break the silence.

"Hi, Hanen. It's good to meet you." She gave me an encouraging smile.

"Hello, Dr. Peters. It's good to meet you too." I replied politely, the nerves evidenced by the slight quiver in my voice.

"Call me Allison. Dr. Peters sounds so stuffy," she laughed. "Why don't I tell you a little bit about myself? That way, you can decide if you feel comfortable enough with me to tell me about yourself." Allison gave me another smile.

"Thank you. That sounds good." I responded, still picking at the invisible lint on my pants.

"Well, let's see… I am forty-seven and have been a therapist for twenty-one years. I love my job. It is my passion. I became a therapist because of something that happened to my best friend when I was a girl. I couldn't help her then, but I decided to do what I could to help others when I grew up. I don't usually share so much with my patients, but I have a feeling that you need to know why I'm here." She caught my eyes and continued, "I am married but don't have any kids. I do have a small tribe of nieces and nephews that I adore and spoil any chance that I get. For fun, I garden, read, and skydive." She laughed at my surprised gasp. "Yeah, most people don't take me for a skydiver. But I love it. I just became a certified skydiving instructor."

"Wow. That's impressive," I responded, genuinely impressed. We chatted about nothing important for the next few minutes.

"Before we continue, I want to explain something critical to you. The relationship between a therapist and their patients is based on trust, openness, and honesty. I can only help someone who allows me to. Because of this, it is very important that my patients feel comfortable with me. If you are uncomfortable, I will not be offended if you look for another therapist. The most important thing to me is finding someone you feel you can talk to. I need you to promise to be honest and look for another therapist if you ever feel you can't trust me. And I promise you that I will always be honest with you and keep anything you share confidential. The only exception is if I feel you are a threat to yourself or someone else. Then I legally have to inform someone."

"I understand," I responded.

"Would you like to tell me a bit about yourself? "

"Yes," I took a deep breath and then continued. "I am thirty-nine years old. I was born in Baghdad and came to Canada after I married my husband fifteen years ago. I have a beautiful daughter, Hamsa, and a handsome son, Hamid. My husband is amazing. Allah has blessed me."

"It sounds like you are indeed blessed. Do you work outside the house?"

"I work as a receptionist at a doctor's office. But I am considering getting a job as a teacher. It is what I am trained in." I explained.

"Many women choose to stay home when their child is small. It is nice that you have been able to do that. A teacher? That is a great job. When you are ready to go to work, I have no doubt you will find a good position," she encouraged me.

"I am nervous about working here because things are very different than in Iraq. I'm afraid I'll make a mistake." I admitted shyly.

"I think you will do amazingly well. But everyone makes mistakes, Hanen. It is part of being human. Even if you do make a mistake, you will learn from it and go on. Most people are kind and understanding. Don't let your fear of making a mistake hold you back." She smiled kindly at me.

"I know you're right. I hate making mistakes. Last night I almost burned the scallops and had a meltdown in front of my friend Allisa.

She teased me, which got me out of my head, and the scallops turned out fine." I laughed at myself a bit.

"What's the worst thing that would have happened if you did burn the scallops?" Allison asked me.

"I would have been embarrassed that my husband had to eat burned food. I don't want to be a bad wife to him."

"Would he have been angry if dinner was burned?"

"Akmal, angry? No, he is beyond kind to me. I just worry that I will let him down. He deserves a better wife than I am."

"It sounds to me like you are a great wife to him. Why do you feel like you aren't?" Allison looked at me questioningly.

I shifted uncomfortably in my seat.

Sensing my discomfort, "If you don't want to answer, you don't have to. This is our first session, and you may not be comfortable with me yet. I would encourage you to think about why you feel like a bad wife when it is obvious that you are a very caring and loving wife."

I gave her a small smile and nodded my head. I was not ready to tell her I knew why I was an unworthy wife.

Another few minutes passed with us talking about mundane things, and then my time was up.

"Hanen, if you would like to meet with me next week, I would like my assistant to schedule you again."

"Yes, I would like that."

"Great. I'll see you in a week. I look forward to getting to know you more."

***

The next Wednesday, I sit on the same brown couch, and Allison is in her blue chair. I noticed a small notebook and a pencil sitting on the side table between us.

"Good afternoon, Hanen. I hope you had a good week. It's good to see you again."

"Hi. It's good to see you too." I reply.

"Before we start, I want to ask if taking notes during today's session would be okay. No one besides me will see them. I lock all my notes in my filing cabinet after each session." She explains.

"It's fine if you take notes," I say.

"Okay, good. Then let's begin. Last week we got to know each other a bit. This week I'd like to explore why you decided to start therapy. You can tell me as little or as much as you are comfortable telling me.", she adds, noticing my leg bouncing in my discomfort.

"Alright…" I stop and think about how to begin. "A few weeks ago, I had an episode when my husband brought me out for my birthday."

"What kind of episode did you have? Can you explain to me how you felt?" Allison is scribbling notes in her notebook and looking up at me occasionally. The fact she isn't just staring at me makes me feel more at ease.

"Well, umm, I got kind of dizzy and couldn't breathe. Then I threw up."

"How long did this last?"

"I guess an hour or so. I felt better the next day when I woke up.

It was embarrassing to have a fit like that." I admit and blush.

"I don't think you had a fit. It sounds to me like you had a pretty intense panic attack. Has this ever happened before?"

"That's a panic attack? I never knew that. I always felt like I was just being overly dramatic. They've happened a few times over the years, but I hadn't had one before that one on my birthday."

"Do you know when it started? What caused it? We call the cause a trigger. Do you know what triggered your panic attack?"

"Yeah, I know."

"Do you feel comfortable sharing with me what that trigger was?"

"I guess…" I pause, take a deep breath, and continue, "My husband's kiss started it. That and the moon."

"Has your husband's kiss triggered you before?"

"No, not usually. It was the way his breath smelled like laban." "I see. Does the moon usually trigger you?"

"No. It was because it was red, like a giant red eyeball looking at me. It reminded me of a moon I saw as a young girl."

"So, the smell of your husband's breath and the red moon triggered you. Usually, when things like that trigger us, they are connected to something we saw or experienced in the past. Are you comfortable telling me what those two things reminded you of?" Allison gently asks.

"I don't want to discuss it, but I need to. That's why I'm here. Well, mostly, I'm here because I promised my best friend I would come, but this is why she made me promise." I inhale and begin. "The smell and the moon reminded me of the first time my uncle molested me when I was six years old." I rush the words out and then give a relieved sigh. I did it. I told her. Now I could start getting better.

CHAPTER SEVEN

Stolen Childhood

8 years old, Baghdad, Iraq

I sat with my elbow on my desk, leaning my head against my hand. My eyelids were heavy, and I found it difficult to focus on anything Mrs. Rasha said. I was just so exhausted.

Last night, while visiting my grandpa's house, Makhi asked my mom if I could stay the night. I said I wanted to go home because I was tired, but they insisted. Later I tried pretending to be asleep, as I often did when he awoke me at night. It rarely worked, and last night was no exception.

Later that night, when he had finished with me, tears flowed freely down my cheeks as I lay on my mat. I wept silently, afraid to wake the others. I was so tired of forcing myself to smile and pretend to be the joking happy girl I'd been before. I was filled with so much pain and anger. Why didn't they see it?

I wanted things to return to how they were before he started making me play these games. I missed the Uncle Makhi, who put me on his bike and peddled me to the ice cream shop. The one who played marbles and soccer with me and picked overflowing baskets of dates.

I prayed, begging Allah to make Makhi stop. Begging him to take away my pain and anger. Pleading with him to make me pure again. The light was creeping onto the horizon before I fell asleep.

***

"Hanen!"

I jumped and looked around, confused. After a moment, I realized I was in my classroom, and Mrs. Rasha stood over me, frowning. All around me, my classmates were laughing and snickering at me.

"Hanen, is it too much to ask that you stay awake in class and sleep at home?"

I was angry. Lack of sleep made me irritable. So I replied sarcastically, "Is it too much to ask that you make class interesting?"

The other students gasped at my audacity, and the laughter instantly died down. Mrs. Rasha jumped backward as though I had slapped her. She gripped my forearm and pulled me to my feet, then half-dragged me to the back of the room. She forced me down into a desk that faced the back wall. She used this to punish students, though why staring at the wall and not having to listen to Mrs. Rasha's droning voice was a punishment, I didn't know. I was much happier to sit back here and drift back to sleep.

"Sit here!" Mrs. Rasha barked. "I will send your mother a note home after school today."

Great. That was just what I needed. Mom already made life difficult on a good day. How would she react when she found out about my latest infraction?

I spent the rest of the day nodding off in the chair, only waking when Mrs. Rasha barked my name and told me to sit straight.

After class, Mrs. Rasha called me to the front of the room. She frowned and handed me a handwritten letter. "Please bring this to your mother and tell her I need to speak with her immediately about your behavior."

I took the note and nodded contritely. "I will. I'm sorry, Mrs. Rasha."

I walked out of school, my head bowed, but as soon as I turned the corner, I straightened and walked faster. I crumpled the note and tossed it away.

A moment later, Bazya caught up to me. At seven years old, she was taller now than I was but thinner and lankier. "What was that, Hanen?" she asked.

"Nothing," I said dismissively. "Nothing? What did it say?"

"Nothing!" I snapped. "Leave me alone."

Bazya pouted. "What's gotten into you? Why are you so mopey all the time? You used to be fun."

"And you used to be cute. Now, look at us."

Bazya giggled. She ran in front of me and walked backward in front of me, batting her eyelashes. "You don't think I'm cute, Hana?"

Despite myself, I started to laugh at her hijinks. Bazya grinned and lifted her hands to her cheeks, opening her eyes wide to look as adorable as possible. "Hana, tell me I'm cute!"

"You're annoying is what you are," I retorted, grinning.

"You're annoying!" Bazya fired back. "Always moping and always sleepy. You're like Dad, except not nearly as pretty."

I playfully swiped at Bazya, who dodged and ran off, laughing. I chased her, calling, "You better hope I don't catch you!"

I sprinted as fast as I could, but Bazya was taller and lighter and easily beat me home. Puffing, we walked through the door into the tarma.

Bazya's hijab was already off when I entered behind her, and her long chestnut brown hair fell in wavy tresses down her back. She was going to be beautiful, I thought. I thought it was a strange thing for someone my age to realize. I was only eight, but I thought many thoughts that would have been more appropriate for an adult.

Seeing how beautiful Bazya was growing increased my worry that Makhi would begin his "games" with her. I had begged him over and over to leave my sisters alone. I promised he could use my body for his needs, even if I had to do more. After all, I was already filthy, soiled, and impure. I needed to protect my sisters at all costs. They should never have to know the twisted feelings of hate, pain, and even forbidden pleasure Makhi brought me. All the emotions overwhelmed me to the point that I could barely function. I hated myself. I hated my life. If suicide were not the ultimate sin, I would have killed myself years ago.

I was so wrapped up in my thoughts I almost didn't see the soccer ball headed straight for my face. At the last second, I looked up and barely managed to sidestep before the ball sailed past me to bounce off the wall of the tarma. I caught it with my heel, grinning as Bazya hopped around and waited for me to pass it back.

We kicked the soccer ball around for a while, just the two of us. My spirits lifted as I played with my sister. These games we played were the only times I felt like a real kid. I used to want to feel like a grownup, but now I would give anything to be carefree like Bazya.

After a while, some of our classmates arrived, calling over the wall for us to come and play. We sprinted for the door, stopping when Mother called, "Hijabs!" We quickly replaced our headgear, then ran outside to play.

Seven or eight other kids were waiting to play, and soon, we had an impromptu match in the street in front of our house. We tried keeping score for a while, but eventually, we lost track and just ran around passing the ball and shooting at the "goals." One was composed of two trash bins stacked close together, and the other was a poplar that grew on one side of the road.

We played through the afternoon. I forgot about my earlier trouble at school and Uncle Makhi's games. Bazya and I ended up on the same team, and we each scored a goal, though, by that point, no one was keeping score anymore. When Mother finally called us in for dinner, we were both flushed and sweaty with exertion but smiling and laughing wildly.

"Look at you two!" Mother exclaimed when she saw us. "Sweating like animals! Go wash up! Your father will be home anytime, and I won't have him coming home to daughters who smell like a pigsty!"

"Yes, Mom," I said, still smiling. I was too happy to let Mother's scolding bother me.

I started toward the washroom, but Bazya brushed past her. "Race you!" she called over her shoulder.

"Hey!" I raced after Bazya, but once again, she outpaced me, reaching the washroom and slamming the door shut before I reached it.

"Hanen!" Mother called down the hall. "Stop slamming doors!" "It wasn't me!" I protested. "It was Bazya!"

"Enough! If you can't behave like a lady, there'll be no dessert for you."

I rolled my eyes and didn't answer. Mom always wanted to blame me for everything, even if it wasn't my fault. I waited outside the washroom until Bazya finished, then began cleaning up for dinner.

I began to wash up, but the washroom was forever tainted. No matter how hard I scrubbed, I always felt dirtier than before I went in.

I flashed back to the last time all my uncles had visited. I needed to wash up before dinner that day as well. As I wrapped a towel around my small body after showering, Makhi quickly snuck in and closed the door behind him.

He reached for me, trying to kiss my lips and remove my towel simultaneously.

"What are you doing? Someone is going to see us!" I tried to push him back to the door, terrified we would be caught.

"Hana, my precious girl, no one will find out. Just be quiet and give me a quick kiss. You know that I need your kisses." He gave me a cajoling smile that always made my stomach turn.

"You must go before they notice you are gone." I pleaded with him.

"I'll leave for you, my precious girl." He gave me a quick kiss on the lips and slipped back out of the washroom.

The memory had me breathing heavily, pushing my fingernails into the flesh of my arm, drawing blood. My good mood had vanished, replaced once more with anxiety and guilt.

There was a loud knock on the door, causing me to jump. "Hanen!" Mother's voice called. "Enough time in the bathroom. Dinner is ready, and everyone's waiting on you!"

"Coming!" I called through the door. I dressed quickly and returned to the dining room, where Father sat beside Mother. He looked up and smiled when he saw me. "Hanen!" he said. "Come, sit with me."

Instantly, my spirits soared again. I smiled and ran to my father's side, throwing my arms around him.

"All right, that's enough," Mother said. "You'll knock over your soup."

"Oh, let the girl hug her father," Grandma chided from mother's other side. "She misses him."

Mother's jaw clenched, and her eyes shot daggers at Grandmother, but she fell silent. She didn't protest further as I continued to hug Father.

I finally released him and sat down to eat. I smiled brightly and asked, "How was your work?"

Father's smile faded, and I worried I may have upset him, but he answered quickly, "Oh, it was all right. The usual boring stuff. Nothing a young woman like yourself needs to worry about." He smiled at me gently. "How was school?"

I shrugged, trying to appear nonchalant. "Eh, nothing special."

"What did you learn?"

I shrugged again. The truth was, I couldn't remember anything that happened today other than the incident with Mrs. Rasha, and I wasn't about to tell my father about that.

"Answer your father," Mother said. "What are you learning?"

I blinked, trying desperately to devise a lie my parents would believe. Bazya came to my rescue, saying, "In my class, we learned about the water cycle today! Did you know that rain comes from lakes and rivers and oceans?"

"Really?" Father said, raising his eyebrow. "I thought it came from clouds."

"Well, yeah, but clouds come from water that evaporates from the surface, like rivers and lakes and ponds and stuff."

"Oh," Father said, nodding understanding. "I see. So, water evaporates from rivers like the Tigris and Euphrates. Then it falls down to the earth from clouds and returns to the river."

Bazya nodded. "Not all of it, though. Some of it sinks into the ground and feeds plants; some runs into ponds and stuff."

"Well, if that's so, then why don't the rivers eventually shrink and dry up?"

Bazya opened her mouth and closed it. She cocked her head to one side. "I don't know," she admitted. "I guess I can ask my teacher about it tomorrow."

Father smiled. "That sounds like a great idea. Make sure you tell me what she says."

"I will!"

Father turned to Shameera. "And how is my beautiful eldest daughter today?"

"I'm well, Father," Shameera answered in what Hanen thought was an unnecessarily formal tone.

"Shameera is growing up," Grandma Khadija said. "At fourteen, she will be ready to marry soon."

"None of my precious girls will be getting married! I'll kill any boy who tries to set foot in this house," Father said jokingly. "Besides, they need to get their education first."

Momma nodded in agreement, "Yes, our girls will be educated. I don't want them to end up married and raising children without going to university and receiving their education."

"But Papa, you will be stuck with us forever if we don't get married," I teased.

"All the better," Father replied playfully. "No man is good enough for my beautiful daughters. Each of you is a gift to me from Allah," he said in all seriousness.

"But what if I don't want to go to university? I don't like school," I said quietly, ashamed of how hard I found it to memorize my history lessons.

"It is important that you have the education to work if your family needs the money. But more importantly, education gives you a better understanding of the world." Father tried to explain.

"If Hanen doesn't want an education, then she shouldn't have to have it. A woman's place is in the house, caring for her family. It is the will of Allah." Grandma interjected.

"This is not up for discussion. Our girls will be educated." My father rarely spoke up, but the matter was settled when he did.

I smiled. I loved my father; he was such a good man. He worked hard to provide for us and would eat dinner when he came home. Our family dinners were wonderful. We laughed and joked together. When he got home too late to have dinner with us, he still spent time with us. He was a man of few words, but the words he did say were wise and full of love. "Hana, talk less and listen more. This is how you grow wise and will please Allah," he often told me.

That night, as I lay on my mat trying to sleep, I prayed that Allah would forgive me for being impure and for my sins with Makhi. I begged that he would stop Makhi from hurting me. And that he would give me a good man like my father for a husband, even though I was sullied and sinful.

***

Present Day, Alberta, Canada, Allison's Office

"Hanen, did you know that it is normal for children who are sexually abused to struggle or even fail in school? In his 1998 book, *Legal Issues in Child Abuse and Neglect Practice,* John Mayer explains why this is so common. Sexually abused children are seriously anxious, frightened, and depressed. These feelings often lead to misbehaving at school. Sexual abuse can cause emotional and cognitive impairments, seriously affecting a child's ability to concentrate in school and causing them to receive bad marks or even fail classes.

Not only that, but sexual abuse can also make children feel numb or disconnected. This lack of emotional engagement makes them feel apathetic and not care about anything.

Unfortunately, too many teachers and school counselors focus on the behaviors and completely miss the abuse causing them. Instead, the child is disciplined, which further traumatizes them and leads to them having even less self-esteem."

The tears flowed freely down my cheeks. It seemed I was always crying these days. For years I had placed my sadness, fear, anger, pain, and depression behind a meters-thick dam. Now that the dam had burst, I felt everything at once.

I thought about what Allison had said. I was not slow or stupid. I was too overwhelmed with what was happening to me to have any ability to focus or achieve in school.

"Are you saying that sexual abuse can actually cause learning delays and cognitive issues?" I asked, not fully believing that the problem wasn't me.

"Exactly. Abused children show higher incidences of ADHD, dyslexia, adaptive social behaviors, etc. Children like you are not weak, Hanen. You are incredibly strong and resilient to have endured all the pain and suffering and survived. You need to remember that you not only survived, but you have thrived! And that is due solely to your strength and resilience. Don't judge the little girl you were. Instead, recognize that her strength allowed you to become the woman you are today and thank her." Allison smiled gently, reached across the space between us, and touched my shoulder comfortingly.

I was surprised that I didn't pull away from her touch. Instead, I returned a wobbly smile as I tried to process everything she had shared.

"I know that we have covered a lot today. For your homework this week, I want you to write a thank you letter to your younger self. Acknowledge her strength and intelligence or whatever you feel like saying. But you must reshape your view of the little girl you were.

We'll meet again next week at the same time. You are doing a great job of working through all this, Hanen. I know it is hard, but you are working to heal yourself."

"Thank you, Allison. I appreciate you saying that."

"You're welcome. It is nothing but the truth. Until next time."

I left Allison's office, my mind racing with unfamiliar thoughts. All these years, I felt stupid because of my academic struggles. Now I find out it was all my mind's way of protecting me. I wasn't sure what it meant, but I knew something fundamental was shifting within me.

"Ugh!" I crumpled up another piece of paper and threw it towards the small rubbish bin in the corner. It was overflowing with wadded-up paper, exactly like the one I had just tossed at it. Normally, the bin would be emptied every day. The idea of an overflowing rubbish bin would have driven me crazy just a few weeks ago. Now I had too much else to think about. The state of the rubbish bin barely registered.

I had tried to write a thank you letter to my younger self all week. And I had probably used a small forest's worth of trees from all the wasted paper. I didn't expect it to be so hard. It seemed like an easy enough assignment. Just say thank you.

"Ugh!" I groaned again and pulled another sheet of stationery from the pile next to me. Let's try this again.

***

"Dear Hanen,

I am future you. I'm thirty-nine and live in Canada with my husband, daughter, and son. Yes, we did manage to leave Iraq. You, me, us…this is confusing. *We* marry a very good man. He treats us with gentleness, respect, and love. Our daughter, Hamsa, is twelve years old, beautiful, smart, and sassy. She is brave; nothing scares her. She also loves her brother, Hamid. Though she would never admit it aloud. Our son is such a handsome boy. He is ten and loves riding his bike, playing video games, and annoying his sister. All in all, we have a wonderful life.

But I am still haunted by what happened to me/ you all those years ago. I kind of had a breakdown on my birthday. I finally told Sama about what Mahki did to us.

She was amazing. She didn't judge us at all! Instead, she cried with me and told me to tell Akmal, our husband's name, about it too.

I'm writing you because my therapist, Allison, told me to. I honestly don't know what to say to you. I keep rewriting this, but therapy is this afternoon, so this must be the last try.

Hanen, you are in so much pain right now, and no one sees it.

You feel alone, angry, depressed, and betrayed.

I wish I could tell you that this pain will end soon. I wish I could return as an adult and fix everything for you, but I can't.

For so many years, I have hated you. I judged you as stupid, dirty, unworthy, and unclean. It was easier to blame you than to deal with all that pain and trauma.

But Hanen, I now know that it wasn't your fault. It wasn't your sin. You were sinned against. You were abused. You were unseen.

Despite all of that, you were strong. You endured, you survived, and you got us out.

Thank you, young Hanen. You are amazing, beautiful, and strong.

Hang in there, Hanen. We have an amazing life ahead of us.

Love,

Your Older Self"

CHAPTER EIGHT

Pick-up Sticks!

10 years old, Baghdad, Iraq

Makhi groaned and shuddered. His grip on my head tightened briefly, then relaxed. He stepped back and began to dress.

I stood still, staring at the wall as I usually did. Makhi was visiting for a week and had awakened me four nights in a row for our little "adventures." My mouth curled into a bitter smile. Once, when I was a little girl, I looked forward to adventures with Makhi. Of course, those adventures included bike rides, walks, and games—normal games like hide-and-seek and hopscotch. Our adventures now were altogether different. It had been a long time since Makhi, and I had enjoyed a "normal" adventure. I wasn't sure they could even be called normal anymore since they existed mostly in my memory.

"Thank you, Hana," Makhi said when he had dressed. As though thanking me somehow made things better. He cleaned himself off and leaned down to kiss me. But I turned away. He paused a moment, then left the washroom.

I was now alone and could begin my ritual of cleansing myself repeatedly. But no amount of scrubbing would ever make me clean. I felt dirty down to my very soul. I hated all of this; I hated my life! I wanted to scream until I had no voice, breaking everything in my rage. I hated Mahki most of all!

No, that wasn't true. I still loved Makhi. He was my uncle. Even though most of the time we were alone, he hurt me. He was still kind and talked to me like I was an adult, not a child.

At first, how he treated me as an equal made me feel special, but I realized how wrong his behavior was as I got older. I wondered if maybe he saw me as an adult only in body and not mind.

No, that couldn't be true, I thought, regarding my small body in the mirror. I was barely ten years old. My body was still not developed as a woman. Anyone looking at my body would see a young girl, so Makhi's attraction to me must have at least a little to do with my maturity.

I thought that would make me feel better, but it didn't. I felt alienated from other kids my age. Other kids enjoyed games, played with toys, or spent time with friends, doing things normal kids did. I pretended to do those things too, but I couldn't enjoy them the same way anymore. In the back of my mind, I knew that no matter how much fun I was having at the moment, I would soon have to follow Makhi to the washroom. My inner turmoil and pain made me angry and sullen. The other children rarely wanted to play with me anymore. Even Bazya didn't spend as much time with me.

I left the washroom and returned to the roof, where everyone slept. I lay awake a while, as usual, and thought about what Makhi had just done to me. Why did Makhi enjoy this so much? It's not like we could do much together. I was still too small to have sex. I shouldn't even know what sex was, but he had ripped that innocence from me long ago. Everything he did and made me do to him, he could do using his own hand. He wasn't a good-looking man, but if he needed a woman to help him, I was sure he could find one closer to his age.

Once when he was visiting and the other kids were doing homework inside the house, I went outside and found him sitting in the tarma, reading. I sat beside him, and he smiled and put his book down. "Hello, Hana. What are you up to?"

"Uncle Makhi, why don't you find a girlfriend your age?" I asked frankly.

His smile faded briefly but returned a moment later. He brushed my hair behind my ear and whispered so no one could overhear, "Maybe I just like you better than other girls."

"How?" I wondered. "You can't even really have sex with me."

He started then and glanced around to ensure no one was near enough to overhear. "Hana," he said, leaning close and whispering. "You mustn't talk like that."

"Why?" I asked again, refusing to lower my voice.

"Because other people won't understand what we have," he said.

"You mean other people won't understand why a grown man likes a child and not a grown woman?"

"Hana, stop it!" he cried, looking around again.

His face was white with fear, and I smiled perversely, enjoying the fact that he was the one who was uncomfortable for once. My grin widened, and I continued to taunt him. "Do other women not like it?"

"Shut up!" he hissed, gripping my slight shoulders until I winced. He relaxed his grip and said, "I like you, Hana, that's all. That's why I… do things with you and not other girls. If you don't like it, that's fine. I won't do it anymore."

"Okay," I said, still grinning wildly. "I don't want you to do it anymore!" I laughed and left him there, feeling better than I had in years.

Makhi hadn't touched me the next two times he visited. I started to hope my nightmare had come to an end. He hadn't touched me until tonight.

I closed my eyes, and only when my cheeks felt wet did, I realize I was crying.

***

The next day I ran ahead of my sisters when school let out. I was glad to be done. I needed a few minutes by myself to shake the memory of the night before, to try and free myself from its stain, if only for a few minutes.

After changing out of my school clothes, removing my hijab, and grabbing a quick snack, I ran outside and climbed on the wooden swing that hung in the tarma.

I pumped my legs as hard as I could, and soon I was soaring high into the sky, the wind blowing my long, dark hair everywhere, wisps flying in front of my face. I loved this swing. While I soared through the air, with the sunlight warming my skin, I felt like a child again, free and happy. These brief moments of normality were precious to me. I stored their memories like precious gems, pulling them out to remind me of better times when the darkness began to overwhelm me.

***

"Hanen!"

I bolted upright, gasping.

Bazya pointed and laughed, and my cheeks reddened. "You scared me!" I cried.

"Your face!" Bazya said. "You should have seen your face!"

I reached out to grab her, but she dodged, still laughing, and said, "Hey, you're the one that wants to sleep until ten on the first day of Eid."

I blinked. Eid. Suddenly, I was bouncing with excitement. Eid! Today was the start of Eid! As usual, we were visiting my uncles' house for the holiday.

I leaped up and squealed with excitement. Bazya joined me, and we jumped up and down, thinking of the delicious treats that awaited us.

The first day of Eid al-Fiter was a feast day, the first day after Ramadan, and possibly the most exciting day of the year for my sisters and me. There was food! So much food! Bryani, laban, masgouf, fresh-baked samoon served while it was still steaming, daheen, kleicha, quzi, the list went on. My uncles had spent the previous day gathering apples, oranges, tangerines, and grapes from the orchard. They then set the table with a huge array of fruit for the children to snack on throughout the day, along with cheeses, cured meats, and flatbreads.

I raced downstairs, making it halfway before I realized that I was still in my night clothes. I raced back up, nearly running over my sister, who was on her way down. "Sorry!" I called over my shoulder as I raced up and changed quickly into my dress. I didn't bother with the hijab. For Eid, everyone stayed home to enjoy their own feasts. So, I wouldn't leave the tarma today. I ran downstairs, where my mom, dad, and uncles waited.

Mother smiled and said, "Good morning, Hanen." Everyone was in a good mood on Eid.

I hugged my mom and kissed her on the cheek, then ran to my father and kissed him briefly. My grandmother entered, and I hugged her before rushing to the table and selecting the best-looking tangerine I could find.

"What, uncles don't get hugs?" Nasir protested, smiling.

"Hug!" I shouted playfully, peeling the tangerine and popping a section into my mouth. As the sweet, tangy fruit enveloped my tastebuds, my eyes rolled with pleasure. I could hear the adults laughing at me, but I didn't care.

After finishing the tangerine, I grabbed a handful of grapes and popped them into my mouth one by one. "Hey, save room for the daheen," Father reminded me.

"You mean save room for dinner," Mother corrected. "That too," he laughed.

"Trust me, I'll be able to eat dinner," I promised, prompting more laughter from the adults.

Bazya poked her head inside. "There you are!" she said. "Come outside. Makhi's teaching us to play pick-up sticks."

"Pick-up sticks?" Father asked. "What's that?"

"It's an American game!" Bazya said excitedly, "One of his friends from the University gave it to him."

"Makhi sees enough of me," I said. "I'm eating."

I grabbed a piece of cheese, wolfed it down, and reached for an apple. My grandmother stopped me, still laughing. "Go play with your sister," she said. "There will be plenty left when you come back inside."

I grinned at Khadija. "Not if I eat it all first," I said. I grabbed the apple and ran outside, popping it into my mouth and biting a huge chunk when I reached the tarma. Shameera stood under the shade of the lemon tree, holding Zayna. My youngest sister, barely three months old, looked around wide-eyed. Makhi was kneeling in front of Bazya and explaining what the different stick colors meant. He looked up and smiled when he saw me. "Hello, Hanan," he said. "Are you coming to play with us?"

I nodded. "Yep. I just needed first dibs on the snacks." I took another bite of the apple and looked at the pile of sticks on the ground. "So, what do we do?"

"Well, the goal of this game is to earn as many points as possible."

I rolled my eyes. "That's the goal of most games, Uncle Makhi,"I chided.

Bazya and Shameera snickered, and Makhi rolled his eyes back at me. "All right, Hana. The goal of this game is to earn points by carefully removing sticks from the pile without moving any of the other sticks."

I wrinkled my nose. "It sounds boring."

"You sound boring," Makhi retorted. "The yellow sticks are each worth one point. The red sticks are worth three points. The blue sticks are worth five points; removing the black stick is worth twenty points."

"What do you get if you win?" Bazya asked.

Makhi looked at her. "What is the matter with you girls? Does everything have to involve a prize? You win the game if you win!"

Bazya's brow furrowed. "Hana's right. This does sound boring."

Makhi rolled his eyes again. "Well, if you don't want to play, that's fine. Shameera and I can enjoy a lovely morning together while you two stuff your faces some more."

Bazya laughed. "I'm just teasing, Uncle Makhi. Of course, I want to play."

Makhi grinned. "All right but watch it with the attitude. You're both far too young to be so bold."

"My age has never mattered to you before," I quipped. Realizing what I said, I gasped and felt the tension in my chest.

I didn't intend to say it, but the words came out anyway.

Makhi's smile faltered for an instant, but he recovered quickly. "All right. To start, I'll drop the sticks. Wherever they land is where we'll start." He lifted the sticks a foot or two off the ground and released them. They fell into a disorganized pile except for the black stick. It somehow separated from the rest and rolled several feet away, finally coming to rest next to the trunk of an apple tree. I walked slowly over and picked it up, studying it. The stick was made of balsa, making it light and fragile. I stared at it, fascinated at the deep black color. The wood was natural, but the color wasn't. It wasn't the soft, light tan of balsa but the deep heavy black of night, a night with no stars to break up the never-ending darkness.

I wondered if the wood had a memory of the tree it once was— tall and proud. Could it feel the change on some level as it was cut down, whittled away, and stained until what was a tall, green, living thing was now only a splinter of wood, black as obsidian? I wondered if it was also black on the inside or only on the surface. I held the stick between my thumb and forefinger and snapped it in half. How easily it broke! The inside wasn't a deep black like the surface, but the stain had permeated through, mixing with the wood's natural color and leaving it a dirty, mottled gray. Tiny veins of black snaked through the wood as though reaching for any last vestige of light that it could ruin.

"Hanen!" Makhi called.

I blinked and turned around. He stood over me with an oddly satisfying expression of disappointment, irritation, and fear.

"Why did you do that, Hanen? You broke it."

"Did I?" I asked. I didn't know why, but the black fascinated me. It seeped into the wood and changed it to gray, but also how the black dye seemed to send tentacles of darkness into the wood, reaching and grabbing for everything the wood once was. I dropped the stick on the ground and left it there, broken, as I walked back into the house without another word.

***

I sat through dinner in a fog. The rest of the family laughed, bantered, and enjoyed themselves as they always did during Eid. The other children included me in their conversations. No one seemed to be angry at me for ruining the game earlier. Eid was far too exciting and joyous for something so small to bother anybody. I didn't feel much relief about that. In fact, I didn't really feel much of anything at all. I couldn't get the tendrils of black in the broken stick out of my mind.

I responded when someone spoke to me and even managed to smile, laugh, and act like nothing was wrong, but it was all an act. I kept feeling the stick break in my hands and seeing the little black veins of the stain working through the wood. In my memory, they seemed to wriggle like living things—little worms that chewed and ate through the balsa.

I ate mechanically because the food was before me, but I didn't taste anything. After dinner, Khadija called me into the kitchen and snuck me an extra square of Daheen.

"It's the best part of the batch," she confided, her eyes twinkling. "I saved it just for you and me. Don't tell anyone, okay?"

I smiled and nodded and made a show of enjoying the sweet, but it tasted like ash in my mouth. I couldn't have told Grandma Khadija how, if at all, it differed from the earlier, similarly flavorless food that I'd eaten.

I felt like I was drifting outside my body, far away from where I was. It was like that black stick rolled away and carried me away with it. I experienced the world as a dream rather than a reality. It was like a dream, but not really, because I never knew I was dreaming when I dreamed. I imagined it would be a nightmare because of the stick and the black veins if I were in a normal dream.

When the food, prayers, and celebrations were finally finished, I welcomed sleep, hoping I would wake in the morning with this strange fog lifted.

***

Present Day: Office of Allison Peters

Allison sat quietly for a moment, processing the memories I had just shared.

"Hanen, why do you think you broke the black pick-up stick," she asks, looking at me as she awaited my response.

"I don't really know. It just made me feel weird when I looked at it."

"Why do you think it made you feel weird? Can you identify the weird feeling it gave you when you looked at it?"

"I guess I was curious about it. I wanted to see if the black dye was on the inside or outside." That weird feeling was encroaching on me again like an evil vignette trying to encircle me, blurring everything around the edges.

"Why were you so curious, do you think?"

"I was a little girl. I was curious about all kinds of things." I shrug, trying to push the feeling of vulnerability away.

"If this conversation makes you uncomfortable, we can leave it for now." Allison gives me a gentle smile.

The smile irritates me, though I try not to show it. She's being kind; she doesn't deserve my ire, I remind myself. I force myself to return her smile, "It's fine. It's only a piece of a child's game," I give a shaky laugh before continuing. "I guess I was curious because balsa wood is such a pretty, light wood; it's fragile. The ink was so black. It felt wrong for such a little stick to be covered in so much black ink. It feels silly to say that." I give a half laugh.

"It isn't silly. Your feelings are your feelings. And they are not silly. One of the things children who suffer long-term abuse learn to do is minimize their feelings. It is one of your brain's defense mechanisms. By disassociating from the feelings of what you are experiencing, your brain allows you to function. Because you were so young when you learned to dismiss your feelings, it became a part of personality development."

Allison pauses for me to interject. I wave for her to continue. This was all new information to me, but it made so much sense!

She nods and continues, "An adult who goes through a traumatic experience has a frame of reference for what "normal" feels like." Allison makes finger quotation marks when she says the word normal. "At six years old, you had not experienced enough life or developed enough of your psyche to know anything else as normal. Your brain's defense mechanisms become an integral part of your personality because those are the years you develop those things. You must learn to value and respect your feelings for the first time. And that is going to feel very weird. But every time you find yourself laughing off something that you are feeling or pushing it away, no matter how small a thing it seems to be, I want you to pause to acknowledge that feeling."

"So, my personality would probably be different if I was never abused?" I ask, emotion threatening to overwhelm me. "I might have been an entirely different person," I ask, trying to get my mind around this new idea.

"Parts of who you are would probably still be the same. For example, you are an incredibly passionate and strong person. Those would still be a part of you, but they might have expressed themselves differently. If just surviving hadn't taken so much of your resources, those parts of your personality would have found other ways to express themselves. You might have channeled them into a hobby or developed a passion for a subject in school and pursued further education. But parts of you would definitely be different. You would find it easier to trust your own judgment. You would probably have an easier time trusting and connecting with others." Allison leans over, handing me a handful of tissues because tears flow unbidden down my face.

"H---he stole s-s-so much from m-me!" I force out through my sobs.

"Yes, he did. But he was the thief, a coward sneaking through in the darkness of night, taking what did not belong to him. Hanen, you were stronger than him. You didn't just survive him. You left him in the dust of his cowardice and built a beautiful life. Allow yourself to be angry with him for what he did. Rant, rage, cuss, throw things. Let it all out, and then move on. Anger is healthy. It is appropriate. But you can't stop at anger. If you do, you will only grow bitter. You won't heal. And Hanen, you deserve to heal." Allison stopped talking and let me sob on her office sofa.

Every few minutes, I stopped sobbing and would rant, "I'll never forgive him! He ruined me! I hate him! I hate my entire family because they just let him do that to me. They let him steal my innocence, my childhood, my very personality! I hate him!"

All the while, Allison sits quietly, letting me get it all out.

After twenty minutes, my sobs finally stopped. I felt more tired and drained than I ever had in my life. I didn't feel this exhausted after delivering my children. I could hardly hold my eyes open. "I'm so sorry!" I apologize, embarrassed by my outburst.

"Don't apologize, Hanen. That was healthy. That was a big step in your healing process. Don't apologize for your feelings. Honor them, make room for them. You are probably exhausted after that. If you are up to it, I want you to think a bit more about why you broke that pick-up stick and write about it sometime this week. Only do it if you are ready."

I sniff and nod, letting her know I understood her, too tired to speak.

"I have another client, so I have to leave. But we are meeting in another room. You sit here as long as you need." She goes to her desk and grabs an unopened box of chocolates from a drawer. "Sometimes, we need a safe place to rest and a little chocolate." She hands me the box and quietly shuts the door behind her as she exits the room. I don't even have a chance to thank her.

***

Throughout the week, I found myself vacillating between rage and heartbreak. I could barely drag myself from my bed.

I woke up with Akmal, made breakfast, and kissed him as he left for work. After he was gone, I awoke, fed, and brought both Hamsa and Hamid to school. Then I would go to work. Allisa picked them up from school because I didn't get off until an hour after they got home. I refused to leave them alone. Hamsa begged me to just let them take the bus. They would be fine on their own for a few minutes. After all, they weren't babies anymore. There was no way she could understand why I protected them the way that I did. I understood that seemingly harmless people could be monsters and refused to leave them unprotected for the world's monsters to prey upon.

Allisa never complained. Without fail, she picked them up from school and brought them home. She would make them do their homework until I got home. I thanked Allah for her friendship every day. She never asked me why I needed her help so much. She just stepped in and cared for my babies like they were her own.

When they left, I would lie in bed and bury myself under the blankets. Some days I would read or try to watch TV. But mostly, I alternated between crying and sleeping.

I would get out of bed in time to quickly straighten the house, shower, and start dinner before the kids and the Akmal arrived home.

I lived this way for most of the next two weeks. The emotional pain was so intense that I felt it in my bones and joints. My grief and pain were so deep that my body grieved with me. I canceled my next therapy appointment, unable to make myself leave my bed.

Finally, two days before the therapy appointment following the one I canceled, I turned my mind to that little black balsa stick and my strange reaction to it.

I grabbed the notebook on my bedside table and began to write anything that came to my head. Not sentences, just whatever words came to me as I visualized that black stick. Dr. Peters called it a "free word association exercise." Whatever that meant.

And now I knew why I hated that little black stick. Hate, I finally named the emotion. I broke that pick-up stick because I hated it. I hated it because it reminded me of myself; fragile, broken, little, and alone.

Poor little Hanen, we deserved so much better.

Chico and Worst Night

11 years old, Baghdad, Iraq

I grinned in anticipation and tried to keep from bouncing on my toes. Bazya had no such inhibition. She jumped up and down like a toddler, squealing and saying, "Daddy, what is it? What is it? What is it?"

Shameera smiled at this display and turned to our mother. She whispered something, and she and Mother laughed before turning back to the younger children. Normally Shameera being this condescending would irritate me. However, today I was too excited to care if she got to pretend to be older than she was. Today it didn't matter.

Tuesday, Bazya complained to Mother that all of her classmates had dogs. Then she begged our parents for a pet. It wasn't true that *all* our classmates had dogs. As far as I knew, of our classmates, only Rahim's and Hassan's families had dogs. I expected Mother and Father to scold her for complaining, but instead, they'd smiled at each other. Then Father had said mysteriously that we were getting a surprise at the end of the week.

Of course, we immediately caught on and spent the next week eagerly awaiting the arrival of our surprise. Friday, I excitedly rushed through my homework. I ran downstairs to meet the others, who waited impatiently for our father to reveal the surprise.

Mother and Father smiled at us as we lined up. I thought it was the happiest I had ever seen my mother. I wondered why she was so happy today when she was usually stressed or angry. However, I had more important things to consider if we got a dog. And as quickly as the thought came, it vanished in the excitement of the surprise.

Finally, Father called, "Makhi! Bring him in!"

Makhi walked in from the hallway, grinning. He held a black- and tan-colored puppy which looked maybe a few months old—big enough to be an armful for Makhi but small enough he could still easily carry him.

Bazya and I squealed with delight. Mother and Father started laughing. Inspired by the excitement around him, the puppy leaped from Makhi's arms and ran toward us, barking and running in circles around everyone. Bazya leaned over and ran after him, arms outstretched to pick him up, but he easily evaded her and stopped to sniff everyone. I felt almost giddy when he pressed his wet nose into my palm.

Is this what falling in love feels like? I thought, then laughed at the silliness of the idea. The more I felt his nose on my palm, the less I cared if it was silly.

"Whatever," I said out loud as I squatted down to pet him. "It feels like love to me."

"What's that?" Father asked.

"Nothing," I said, taking advantage of the puppy's momentary stillness to wrap him in a bear hug. "I just said I love the puppy. Thank you, Daddy."

He smiled. "Of course, princess. I'm glad you like him."

"Of course we like him!" Bazya cried, holding her arms out to catch the puppy as he leaped from my arms. "He's adorable!" She squeezed him to her chest and asked. "What's his name?"

"He doesn't have one yet," Mother said. "We thought you two could name him."

"Really?" Bazya said. "Oh, thank you!" "So?" Makhi asked. "Any thoughts?" "Chico!" Bazya cried.

Makhi grimaced. "Chico? What kind of name is that?" "An awesome name!" Bazya insisted.

I laughed. "Chico sounds perfect."

"What does that even mean?" Makhi asked. "What language is that?"

"It's Spanish!" Bazya explained. "It means boy."

"You want to name your dog after the Spanish word for "boy"?"

Bazya put the puppy down. It promptly resumed its circuit of running and barking and sniffing. She put her hands on her knees and glared at Makhi. "Well, what do you want to name him?"

He blinked. "I…um… well…"

"It's settled!" I exclaimed, putting an end to the argument. "Chico, it is."

Mother grinned at him. "Sorry, Makhi." I felt a strange and unexpected burst of pride that Mother chose our name over whatever Makhi might have wanted. I smiled at my mother, but by then, my father was close, and the two looked at each other with curious, almost happy expressions. That look seemed significant, but I couldn't put my finger on why it would be.

Makhi shrugged. "Eh. As long as it comes when we call."

We played with the puppy for a few more minutes before Mother said, "All right, time to put the puppy outside and get ready for dinner."

"No!" Bazya cried, grabbing Chico and pulling him to her chest. "Just a few more minutes!" I begged. "Please?"

Mother looked like she was about to protest again, but Khadija walked in. "Oh, just let them play with the dog. Dinner will still be there in an hour."

For once, Mother didn't seem displeased at Khadija's correction. She smiled and said, "All right. Just make sure you wash your hands really well before you come to dinner."

I wasn't exactly sure if I heard the last part right because as soon as Mother acquiesced, Bazya and I screamed with delight and ran outside with the dog. Chico followed us, tail wagging rapidly, just as excited as his human owners. I called over my shoulder, "Thank you!" I hurried after him.

We laughed and ran and chased him through the tarma. I felt like a child again, a normal child whose only concerns were homework, chores, and, most of all, play. I felt like a normal girl who could play with recklessness and abandon. I hadn't realized how long it had been since I felt that way or how much I missed it. It felt… it felt *amazing*! As I tossed a stick for Chico to catch, he stopped and cocked his head inquisitively, and I felt a rush of gratitude for my parents. I felt gratitude for Chico, too, for giving me a chance to capture those feelings again.

"He doesn't know fetch yet!" Bazya giggled.

I grinned back at her. "Let's teach him!"

We spent the next twenty minutes unsuccessfully trying to train Chico to fetch. Finally, as the darkness of night began to settle in, Mother called. "Okay, Bazy, Hana, time to come inside."

"Aww," Bazya whined. "Do we have to?"

"Yes, you have to," Mother said tolerantly. "He'll still be here tomorrow when you get home from school."

Father walked outside and called Chico to him. Chico ignored him, and Bazya and I were treated to more entertainment as we watched Daddy run around the tarma, struggling to grab the elusive puppy. We laughed and teased as he lunged and gasped and stumbled after Chico. Finally, he reached him and picked him up, huffing with exhaustion. He noticed us laughing and smiled at us, shaking his head as though exasperated. "He's almost as difficult as you two!" he quipped as he carried the puppy to the shed. I could see a small wire enclosure with water and food bowls inside.

After dinner, Bazya and I asked to see Chico again, but Mother said no. "You two need to get rested for school."

"Please?" Bazya asked, hands clasped in front of her. "Just to say good night?"

Mother sighed and rolled her eyes. "All right, you can say good night. But then—"

I didn't hear the rest because we immediately bolted outside and ran to the shed. Chico ran to us, pushing against the wire. He stood on his hind legs and barked excitedly, tail wagging. He seemed so happy to see us! This was love. This was exactly what love was like. I was sure about that.

We cooed, petted him through the fence, and promised to play with him again in the morning, staying until Mother came to the shed and declared, arms folded, that we had already said good night. It was time to wash for bed. Bayza almost begged for more time, turning her head and opening her mouth. She could see such a request would fall on deaf ears, though, and closed her mouth. I felt like a much older sister for realizing that sooner and not even thinking about asking for more time.

I fell asleep with a smile. My thoughts were so wrapped up in Chico that I forgot all about Makhi. Instead, as sleep gradually overcame thought and I slipped into a calm, sweet slumber, I only felt excitement and happiness. That dog… that was love. I didn't think of Makhi until he shook me awake again.

I sighed but didn't pretend to sleep. I was too excited to have a dog to feel too bad about playing another one of Makhi's games. Maybe he would touch me tonight instead of the other things he made me do. His touching me wasn't so bad. I felt a stab of guilt at the thought. I knew what we were doing was wrong, but if I had to do it anyway, was it so bad to hope he only did the things that felt good instead of the stuff that hurt and made me want to scrub my skin from my body.

I walked to the bathroom; a blind lamb led by a hungry wolf. This night Makhi took away the last shreds of my innocence. The pain, the intense, all-consuming, time-stopping pain. It felt like he was cutting my body in half with a dull sword as he pushed and pulled in and out of what used to be my body. But it wasn't my body anymore. He'd taken the last precious thing that was mine to give the man I married. All my choices had been taken from me; now, he owned my body and soul. We were both smeared with the same inky, black, foul-smelling sin. Push and pull, in and out, his hand pushing hard against my mouth, silencing even my screams of pain. Like everything else, I screamed in silence as he split my body in half and severed my soul from my being.

Afterward, he stood up and refused to look at me or say anything as he dressed. Then he left, leaving me lying on the bathroom floor, bleeding and in more pain than I knew a human could feel. I may have lost consciousness because the next thing I remember is looking around, not fully comprehending where I was.

Then the pain hit again. I felt like someone had shredded my insides with a knife and set them on fire. I bit down on my hand to stop myself from screaming out in pain. I struggled off the bathroom floor and cleaned up the best I could. I thoroughly rinsed the washcloth I used to clean the blood off my body and the floor. Hopefully, no one would ask about it.

Then I stumbled to my bed. Before I could drift off to sleep, I had a terrifying thought; what Mahki and I had done was how babies were made.

Pregnant. Could I get pregnant? I didn't even have real breasts! How could he have… I told him no! And he ignored me! I fought back the anger for a moment. Could I get pregnant? I hadn't had my period yet. Didn't girls have their periods first, and then they could get pregnant?

Another stab of pain ran through me, and I stopped thinking about it. I was too tired. I was so tired. And I hurt everywhere.

I was a whore now. That's what Mrs. Rashid called women who had sex with men other than their husbands. They were whores. They weren't worthy of being wives or mothers but were outcasts. Now I was one of them. "Whore," "Fornicator," I rolled the words around in my mind, getting used to my new identity.

"I'm a fornicator," I whispered.

I wanted to cry, but I couldn't. I could only lay there. Once more, it took the light of dawn to finally give me the strength to gather myself and head back to bed.

The next day my mother saw my bloody sheets and assumed I had begun my monthly cycle. She was kind, giving me pain medicine and a hot water bottle "to help with the cramps," she'd said. I didn't have cramps as she meant, but my body screamed in anguish. I was grateful when the hot water bottle and pain meds lessened the pain enough for me to go back to sleep. Later that day, Makhi stopped in to say hi.

"This is over. You will never touch me again."

He looked down, "You're right. I'm sorry, Hanna. I just love you so much," he said quietly.

"Get out!! NOW!" I screamed at him.

He left the room without saying another word.

***

Present Day, Allison Peters' s Office

"I'm so sorry that happened to you, Hanen. You should never have been abused like that. You didn't deserve it. You were just a little girl." Allison's professional demeanor slips momentarily, and I see tears in her eyes.

"I still feel numb when I talk about that night. I cry over everything else. Why don't I cry over the worst night of my life?"

"Your mind isn't ready to let its defenses down yet. Like you said, it was the worst night of your life. You were deeply traumatized physically, emotionally, and psychologically. Your talking about it tells me you have already made much progress in healing. Give yourself time to process. Your trauma didn't happen overnight, and neither will your healing. Be patient and give yourself grace."

"I've barely left my bed for two weeks. I haven't been able to work. I feel like all I do is sleep, cry, and repeat. I want to be able to function and live my life!" I fiddle with the ends of my hijab, frustrated with myself.

"This is just one step on your healing journey. You won't be like this forever. But it is good for you to get fresh air. I want you to try to take a short walk every day, even if it is only to your mailbox. Fresh air and nature are healing to our souls." Allison gives me one of her signature smiles.

"I'll try," I responded noncommittally.

"Do you feel comfortable enough to talk a bit more about this memory?" She pauses, waiting for me to answer.

I take a few moments to collect my thoughts and evaluate if I have a deeper discussion in me right now.

"I think I'm okay to talk some more," I reply honestly.

"If it gets too much, just tell me, and we will stop. Remember, you control what you talk about or don't." Allison gives me a reassuring pat on my hand.

"Thank you," I say, not knowing how else to respond. "I wanted to talk about your dog."

I looked at her in surprise, "My dog? You want to talk about Chico?"

"Yes. It sounds like he was a wonderful dog, and you had a deep connection with him."

"He was. I loved him so much." I smile as I remember the little scamp.

"I can tell by how you talk about him. Animals, especially dogs, are deeply in tune with their owners' feelings. Dogs offer us a safe place. They don't judge you and don't expect anything from you more than food, water, and love. You seemed to feel that immediately with Chico."

"I never thought about it, but I did. I felt safe enough to act like a kid with him. I never let myself be that free and uninhibited around people."

"I'm glad you had Chico. What struck me about your story is that the night you opened up and let yourself act like a kid, be happy, and love was the night your uncle raped you. He abused you for years but never raped you until that night."

I sat stunned. I'd never put those things together. What did it mean? Why would he do that? My mind swirled with questions I couldn't seem to voice. "It was the only time he ever raped me. Even after that night, he did other stuff to me but never again raped me." I don't know why I needed to explain that to almost defend him. What he did to me had no defense.

"He traumatized you for your entire childhood. He didn't "only rape you once." He abused, traumatized, and raped you. There is no qualifier. Sometimes it is easier to deal with our trauma by minimizing it.""

"I didn't mean to minimize it," I say defensively.

Allison nods and continues, "Abusers have to be in control of their victims. They want to be the center of their victim's universe because they might lose control over them otherwise. I don't think it is a coincidence that your uncle raped you that night. I think it was his way of maintaining control over you. I would wager that he felt threatened by your connection to Chico, which is why he raped you when he did. It was his way of punishing you and maintaining control." Allison looks at me intently.

I have no words. For years I assumed Makhi's lust for me had pushed him too far that night. That he did it to punish me for being happy was a thought I could not process. "You mean he wanted to hurt me. That it wasn't about him needing sex?"

"Rape is never about sex. Rape is always about control. It is an act of violence that comes from a need to overpower another person. It is not ever about a person just wanting sex. Sex is the tool your uncle used to abuse, inflict pain, and manipulate you. None of it came from a place of love or even lust. Those are the words they use to excuse their abuse. But someone who loved you would not have treated you like your uncle treated you."

"Um, I think I need time to work through this. I honestly don't know what to think or feel right now."

"That is perfectly fine. I am so glad you spoke up and told me what you needed. Thank you for trusting me enough to be honest with me."

"You're welcome," I awkwardly mumble.

"I know you have a lot to process. This week I want you to take one short walk a day and continue to journal your thoughts and feelings if you feel up to it. Journaling doesn't have to be an in-depth, time-consuming thing. It can be as simple as jotting down a few sentences when you have feelings or thoughts you want to work through. You can even use your phone to record or write a quick note in your app."

"Thanks, Allison," I say as I leave.

"I mean it when I say you are an incredibly strong and resilient woman. Remember that on the hard days. I'll see you next week."

CHAPTER TEN

Perfect Women

Present Day, Our Apartment

I sat up and sighed, wiping my forehead, which didn't accomplish anything because my hand was just as sweaty. I felt gross and dirty, but at least the flat was getting clean! I took a break and headed into the kitchen to grab some paper towels.

I passed the living room, where Hamsa and Hamid played video games together. "Watch out, there is a reaper behind you!" Hamid exclaimed. "Do you have any diamond armor?" Hamsa asked. I watched them from the hallway for a moment. Minecraft made no sense to me. But they would play for hours if I let them. "Hey, I'm just going to finish the hallway, then I'll come to play a board game with you both, okay?"

"Can we play Monopoly?" Hamsa asked. Monopoly was her favorite board game, probably because she always won. She was ruthless in acquiring properties and slowly bankrupting the rest of us. Hamid sighed. "Can we play something else, anything else? Hamsa is mean when she plays that. She never lets anyone else win!"

"Being competitive is not being mean. If y ou want to win, play better! Right, mom?" Hamsa rubbed salt in the wound.

"How about we read some Harry Potter together?" I say, redirecting the conversation. "We can even eat a couple of Oreos while we read," I sweeten the deal, literally.

"All right!" Hamid exclaimed. He had quite the sweet tooth. "Sounds good to me," Hamsa agreed.

"Looks like supermom saves the day again!" I smiled while thinking to myself.

I gave Hamsa a hug and then chased Hamid around a room. It was an old game that we had started when he was a toddler. I would try to hug him, but he would run away, and I would give him the biggest hug I could when I caught him.

I turned around suddenly, surprised. Akmal lifted his hands placatingly. "Sorry!" he said. "Sorry, I didn't mean to startle you."

Suddenly I remembered the unfinished hallway and quickly let Hamid go. "I'm sorry!" I said. "I got distracted. I'll finish the chores right now."

I hurried to the kitchen, but Akmal caught my shoulders. "Chores? *Habibti*, what are you talking about? The house is spotless!"

"Almost," I replied. "I just have to finish the hall—"

He kissed me softly, stopping me from finishing. "Relax. The house looks beautiful."

"I just don't want you to be embarrassed in front of Kazim and Rabah," I explained. "I want you to be proud of your house."

He chuckled. "If Kazim and Rabah can find fault in this house, then Kazim and Rabah can host dinner next time. I'd love to see them get that… that stable anywhere near the condition this place is in."

"Akmal!" I laughed. "Don't call their house a stable! That's rude!"

"It's true, though," he said. "Of course, it only seems worse because of how perfectly you keep this house. Most hospitals would look like a stable compared to this place."

"Actually, most hospitals are surprisingly dirty. I read online that many places don't even sanitize beds before accepting new patients."

"Don't believe everything you read online," Akmal cautioned with a smile.

"Really?" I tease, folding my arms and smiling sarcastically. "This, coming from you?"

He blushed, and I felt the same giddy rush I always did when I could make him blush. "I'm just saying the house is very clean," he said lamely.

"So, it's just your wife who's dirty," I continue to tease him. "Don't worry, I'll be bright and shiny for your little dinner party."

"When did I say you were dirty?" he asks, exasperated. "I literally just kissed you."

"That doesn't mean anything," I wink. "A man will kiss a cow's backside if she will let him." I was surprised by how much bitterness was in my voice and hoped Akmal would take it as a joke.

"Why so testy today?" Akmal said.

I blanched and was about to apologize, but he smiled when I looked at him. He was just teasing me.

"Oh, Akmal," I sigh, "I just want to be a good wife for you." "*Habibti*," he said. He kissed my forehead. "You're the best wife.

What's going on? Is everything okay?"

"I'm fine!" I laugh. And push away from him. "But I really am dirty. I'm going to go wash up before Kazim and Rabah get here."

"I think you look beautiful," Akmal said.

"I think you're lying," I called behind me, laughing as I walked upstairs. I didn't feel light-hearted anymore, but I tried to make my laugh genuine.

I spent a lot of time in the shower, scrubbing carefully and then scrubbing again until I realized what I was doing. Since my last therapy appointment, I'd been scrubbing more often, just like when I was a girl. I tried to push thoughts about Mahki and the past from my mind as I dried off and put on my clothes. Showered and dressed, I felt a little better, but as I looked in the mirror, I couldn't shake the feeling that this was all an act, that the real me was still a dirty, used, broken girl.

Akmal came in and hugged me from behind. I smiled and fought off the instinctive wave of revulsion at the touch. "My pure Hanen," he murmured softly, kissing my ear. "My lovely, pure Hanen."

Pure Hanen. I felt a powerful rush of guilt. I wasn't pure. I was the furthest thing from it. Poor Akmal. He deserved a real wife, a truly pure wife. He deserved a pure wife and not Makhi's castoff.

I almost shouted, "No!" out loud. I was not Mahki's castoff; I wasn't a whore or a fornicator. I was a strong and resilient woman who survived a monster's torture. I was not unworthy! No more would I allow Mahki's evil to affect how I saw myself. I was a woman worthy of the husband Allah had blessed me with. I was his wife, and he was all the husband any woman could ever hope to have.

"You are so pure and wonderful, Akmal," I smile, "that any wife would seem spotted and soiled by comparison."

"Any but you, my love," he said with a chuckle. He kissed my ear again and said, "But perhaps I'm more lovely. You look better in a dress, but other than that—"

I laughed, "You're incorrigible."

He kissed me and said, "And you're beautiful."

Hamsa and Hamid started to argue over the game, and Akmal let me go so I could settle the argument. I returned to the living room and said, "I think that is enough video games. You can go play something else while I finish my chores. Then we will do something together if there is time before our company arrives."

"The house is perfect," Akmal said from the hallway. "Really, it is. Please don't worry about it, okay?"

I sighed and put Hamid down. "Okay."

He laughed and said, "You're just going to wait until I'm gone and keep cleaning, aren't you?"

I shrugged, "Maybe."

He rolled his eyes. "Allah only knows what you see in me if you can look at this house and still find dirt." When I began to respond, he lifted his hand. "I know, I know, I'm beautiful and perfect. I just feel bad for the house. No matter how hard it tries or how clean it gets, it will never be good enough."

He smiled at me, expecting a jab, but his smile disappeared when he saw the look on my face. "Hey, *Habibti*, I'm just teasing. You can finish the hallway if you want to."

"No," I said more sharply than I intended. "You're right; it's pointless." I forced a smile I didn't feel and said, "I'm just being anxious for no reason." Then I stood on my tiptoes and kissed him. "Go upstairs and shower. I'll feed Hamid, then start on dinner."

Akmal didn't return my smile. "Hanen, what's wrong?"

"Nothing!" I say. My light-hearted tone sounded fake in my ears. "Go get ready. I'll handle things down here."

He didn't move. His expression was serious, and it changed his face. The boyish, cute, dorky Akmal was replaced by the strong, commanding, determined Akmal. I'd seen that face before but never directed at me.

"Hanen, for weeks now, you haven't been yourself. You've been anxious and tense. You're either exhausted or working yourself to exhaustion, even when there's no work to be done. You've acted differently around me, too, almost like you're afraid of me."

His face softened again, but concern softened it, not happiness. "You've… even your showers are different. You're in there for hours sometimes. I just… Please, will you tell me what's wrong?"

I stood silently for a long moment. I wanted to tell Akmal everything. I wanted to tell him about Makhi, the sudden resurgence of my memories of his abuse, and the emotions that came with them. More than anything, I wanted to beg him for his forgiveness and promise to be a faithful, perfect wife for him. Maybe it was time; maybe I was ready.

"You're right. We need to talk but not tonight. Tonight, let's just enjoy our company. Tomorrow Allisa will watch the kids, and we can have our conversation.

"*Habibti*, you're scaring me. Please tell me, are you okay?"

"I'm fine. I promise. I will tell you everything tomorrow. Tonight, I want to enjoy my husband and my guests.

He smiled. "Of course, my love." He pulled away from me and said, "Well, I better go take that shower, or I'm going to stand out like a sore thumb against this perfectly spotless house."

I laughed again and watched him walk up the stairs, smiling tenderly. He was a good man.

***

Kazim laughed uproariously as Akmal continued with his story.

Akmal grinned and leaned forward slightly. He did that whenever people showed interest in his stories. It was one of his many endearing traits.

"So, this kid lifts his hands like he's going to fight me, and I'm like, 'Hey, buddy, I just asked you not to skateboard off the stairs because you could hurt yourself or someone else. Chill out. I'm not looking to fight you!'"

"Oh, man…" Kazim said, wiping tears from his eyes.

"So, he kind of shuffles toward me, and I lift my hands 'cause I'm obviously not going to fight someone over this. He thinks, I don't know, maybe he thinks I'm scared or something because he throws the worst punch I've ever seen, ends up tripping over his own feet and faceplanting on the pavement, rolls over and starts screaming, I mean, literally screaming like his face has been torn off."

"Serves him right," Rabah interjected. "Why would he try to hit you anyway?"

"I don't know; I think he might have been drinking. Anyway, I leaned down to check on him, and he freaked out and started shuffling away all wide-eyed, and I tried not to laugh because the kid basically just beat himself up."

Kazim started laughing again, and Akmal's smile widened. I felt a rush of love for him. He was so cute!

"So, I kept telling him, 'Stop! I'm not trying to hurt you! Do you need medical attention? Dude, it's okay! I'm not even mad at you!'"

"So, what happened?" Rabah asked. "Did you find out why he attacked you?"

Akmal nodded, "So, apparently, the kid was on some sort of new drug going around the high school. I don't know how he even managed to skateboard while high, but his parents showed up and chewed him out." He chuckled. "He looked pretty scared, and I don't blame him! His dad looked ex-military, and he was pissed!"

"So, he attacked you because he was high?"

"Yeah. I guess he told his parents I looked really angry and big. Like my muscles looked bigger than they were," Akmal curled his arm, like he was showing off his muscles, and laughed, "So he tried to fight me and then said I hit him so hard I lifted him off the ground, and he was scared."

"He thought you hit him?"

"Yeah, and then his dad shouted, 'HE DIDN'T HIT YOU, DUMBASS! YOU TRIPPED ON YOUR OWN GODDAMN FEET!'"

Kazim burst into laughter again. I suspected Akmal probably invited them over specifically because he knew Kazim would enjoy his stories.

"Oh, so they saw him," Rabah said.

"Yeah, I guess they were shopping in one of the stores nearby, and they walked out just in time to see him throw his Hail Mary at me. Poor kid. I really did feel bad for him. His dad was pissed!"

The dinner continued in a similar vein. Akmal continued to tell stories, and Kazim continued to laugh as though they were the funniest things he ever heard. Sometimes Rabah and I would listen, and sometimes we would talk about our children—Rabah had a three- year-old and a six-year-old at home with a babysitter—and our husbands, Rabbah's work, their favorite tv shows—the usual small talk.

When everyone finished the main course, I cleared the plates and went to the kitchen to prepare dessert.

I overheard them talking about me as I sliced the peach pie and scooped vanilla ice cream onto each slice.

"You are the luckiest man in the world, Akmal," Kazim said. "Hey!" Rabah exclaimed. "What are you trying to say?"

"I mean, come on, Rabah," Kazim joked. "You're not bad, but when has our house been this clean?"

"Maybe you should clean it yourself, then," Rabah said. "Then I can be the one to sit on the couch and watch football all day."

"They call it soccer here, not football."

"Oh, my mistake," Rabah said sarcastically. "But really, Akmal, you are lucky. Hanen is wonderful. You did well for yourself."

"I am lucky," Akmal agreed. "She is a gift from Allah."

"Congratulations, my friend," Kazim said. "Not everyone is lucky enough to find such a woman."

My eyes welled with tears. They said such kind things! If only they knew. I dabbed my eyes with a paper towel and smiled before returning from the kitchen with dessert.

When sleep finally came, it brought no solace. Only another night of bitter memories.

The next day Allisa arrived to bring Hamsa and Hamid to her house while Akmal and I talked. I was washing dishes when I heard her at the door. I quickly dried my hands on a dish towel and greeted her.

"How can I thank you, Allisa? You have no idea how much I appreciate you taking them so we can talk."

"Hanen, it's no trouble. I love these giant monsters," she winked at Hamsa as she said it.

"I'm not a monster! I'm a princess. Dad told me so!" Hamsa pretended to be indignant.

"Well, if your dad said it, then it is true. You are a beautiful princess monster," Allisa teased.

"Mom, can I go to Nadia's house instead? She likes me and doesn't call me names," Hamsa pleaded between giggles.

"Behave, my beautiful 'amira. Make sure to hide the monster while at Allisa's house." I tease her. "I love you and Hamid with my whole heart!" I gathered them into a big hug and kissed them before they headed out the door.

After they left, I grabbed my journal from my nightstand. As I crossed the floor to head back downstairs, Akmal came out of the bathroom, wrapped in his fluffy, warm, green robe. He looked tired from his long day at work. I gave him a weak smile, and he grabbed me and brought me to his chest. I inhaled, loving the smell, a mixture of his aftershave and deodorant. I snuggled deeper into his embrace, the busy day catching up to me. My life didn't stop just because I was near an emotional breakdown because of my traumatic childhood. I had been up since 6 am caring for the children, cooking, and cleaning. I had finally gathered the courage to apply to the local college to take a few courses next semester. I was tired of putting my dreams on hold out of fear and feeling unworthy.

I hadn't eaten much because my stomach had been churning all day, anticipating our upcoming conversation. My empty stomach only added to my fatigue and nausea.

I squeezed Akmal tighter, afraid this may be the last time he held me. I knew that one of two things would happen after our conversation. He would either divorce me. Even if he forgave me and we stayed married, he almost certainly would never see me the same way. I would never again be his "Pure Hanen."

"Why are you crying, *Habibti*? What has you so sad? You're breaking my heart." He lifted my face, brushed away the tears from my cheeks, and gently kissed my lips.

I pulled back, surprised that I had been crying. I hadn't even felt the tears flowing from my soul to my eyes and down my cheeks.

"Amiri, get dressed and meet me in the living room. I'll explain everything then, I promise." I laid one last kiss on his cheek. He had been a gift from Allah in my life. I never knew a man could be so gentle and loving. When I had to leave, I would treasure our time together.

"We can talk now. We don't have to be so formal and go to the living room." He reached for me again, but I sidestepped him.

"I don't want to have this conversation in here. It doesn't belong in our space. I'll meet you downstairs." I left him with a worried and confused expression on his face. I started down the stairs, straightening my spine with each descending step and pushing down the nausea that threatened to climb my esophagus. I still felt the day's exhaustion, but it was quickly becoming overwhelmed by my nerves.

CHAPTER ELEVEN

Deep Secret Revealing

Present Day, Our Apartment

I went downstairs, made tea, and sat in the living room, waiting for Akmal to join me.

I didn't have to wait long. Within a few minutes, he sat on the sofa beside me. He reached over and grabbed my hand. "*Habibti*, tell me what is weighing so heavily upon your shoulders and is making you sad. Don't you know I will do everything humanly possible to bring a smile to your beautiful face? Tell me how I can help you."

I nodded, squeezed his hand, and began to make our tea. I didn't want tea. My stomach was roiling, and bile rose into my throat, but I needed something to keep my hands busy while I considered how to start the conversation.

"Sit down, Hanen. You don't need to serve me. Just talk to me, *Habibti*."

I handed him his tea, set mine on the coffee table, stood, and began to pace, "Amiri, I don't even know how to tell you this story. It happened so long ago, and yet it is so present today. I don't want to break your heart. I don't want to see the light you get in your eyes when you think of me going out."

"Hanen, I love you. Don't you know nothing will change that? Sit down, my love. Tell me what troubles you. Let me share your burden if you won't let me carry it," he looked directly at me, his eyes imploring me to believe him.

"I don't deserve you. You are too good a man for me," my voice shook with the weight of my emotions.

"My pure, beautiful, Hanen. You deserve a much better man than me. But Allah, in his graciousness, blessed me with the most amazing wife." He put his tea down, stood up, grabbed my hand, led me to the sofa, and pulled me down next to him, never releasing me as if afraid I would fly away.

"You don't understand. But soon you will, and then you will know I spoke only the truth. You deserve a better wife than me." I wiped a tear off my cheek with the back of my hand. Between the nerves and my crying, I found it hard to speak.

"I can see you won't listen to reason. So, tell me this great secret you carry that you think will drive me from you." I could hear the frustration and hurt in his voice because I didn't believe him.

"The story I will tell started many years before I met you. Until our date a few months ago, only two other people knew these things about me. Now Sama and my therapist know as well."

"You have a therapist, *Habibti*? When did you start therapy?" Akmal asked in surprise.

"I s---started a—after my bbbbirthday." I manage between sobs. I held up my hand, signaling I needed a moment to compose myself.

"Of course, Hanen. Whatever you need." He squeezed my hand. I was unsure whether it was reassuring or signaling me to continue.

"You know what it was like to live in Iraq since the war of 1991, the constant fear, lack of food, the dust…everything.

Iraq has such a long and beautiful history. For centuries, it was a leader in mathematics, science, literature, and philosophy. But there weren't even books to teach from when I was in school. My father told us how the libraries had been ransacked, and the books were thrown into the Tigris and the Euphrates, turning them black with ink.

Father started off with a good job, but with each war, jobs became harder and harder to find. Like many families, we became poorer and poorer. Father eventually began to drive a taxi to make ends meet. He was gone most of the time working, and when he came home, he was exhausted. But you know how he is. Like you, he is a good man who loved his family.

I'm not complaining because we had it better than some families. For a treat, Father would sometimes buy those small cans of Pepsi. Remember those? And he would pour a little bit into six cups for us to enjoy." I smile at the memory and pause to gather my thoughts before continuing. "You already know how my grandmother, Khadija, lived with us and criticized my mother and her family. She looked down on them because they were poor and less educated. I was her favorite granddaughter and the pawn she used most effectively against my mother. My mother was a sweet and kind woman who only wanted to do her best as a wife and mother. But all I saw as a child was her weakness because I saw her through my grandmother's eyes. I know you already know most of this, but it is important to remember these things because they explain why I didn't feel like I could talk about what happened to me.

We would celebrate Eid with Grandma Fatima and my mother's brothers. And you've heard the stories about how close Uncle Makhi and I were when I was a very young girl.

He always treated me special. He would take me to get ice cream on his bike, play games, and listen to me as if I were grown. He was my favorite uncle." I start to sob again, dreading telling him the next part of my story. How could he possibly understand and forgive me?

After I cried for a while, I began to speak again, so softly that Akmal had to lean toward me to hear my words, "W-W-WWhen I was six, late one night, while everyone else slept, Mahki woke me up. I was so excited because I-I th-thought he wanted to take me on one of our secret night bike rides or go up on the roof to look at the ssstars." I started to hyperventilate between my sobs, the panic and pain of the past wrapping its ugly fingers around my throat and choking me. Akmal grabbed my hand. "Take a break, *Habibti.* You need to breathe. Put your head between your knees and breathe slowly…. In, one, two, three, four. And out…one, two, three, four." He held my hand and counted my breaths, like when I delivered our babies.

After twenty minutes, I was composed enough to continue. "I didn't resist when Makhi grabbed my hand, put his finger to his lips, and led me from the room. I followed along silently, excited for our next adventure." I paused and pulled my hand from Akmal's, unwilling for the filth of my story to touch him in any way. I pushed the nausea and tears down, steeled my will, and continued, "That night, Mahki had a different game in mind. Instead of going to the tarma or roof, he pulled me into the small bathroom and shut the door…." I had to stop again, my throat felt like it was closing up, and I couldn't breathe. The panic attacks kept hitting me.

I slowed my breathing and waited for my tears to slow, "H---he kkkissed m-me---e, grown-up k-k-kisseddd mme. H-he shoved h-h-his tongue in, in…, in my mouth, and I, I felt like I was chchchoking on it. I tried to push him off me, but he was s-s-s-so m-much b-b-b-bigger. He wa-was nine, nineteen, and I w-w-w-as only six." I choked on my tears. I was a mess with tears all over my face and shirt and my nose running uncontrollably. I grabbed a tissue to wipe off my face and gave myself a moment before continuing.

"Once he was done kissing me, he told me not to tell anyone. That this was our secret, and he could not help himself because he loved me so much and I was so beautiful." I couldn't stop the tears that flowed down my cheeks, and I couldn't look at Akmal, afraid to see the disgust on his face. I rushed to continue the story, not wanting to lose my nerve, "For a little while, whenever he was around, all he did was kiss me, touch me over my clothes, or make me touch him the same way. But before long, we were both doing all kinds of vile things. I hated it. I hated him. But I also loved him and knew he was only doing these things because I made him by causing him to lust after me. I h-h-h-hated myself most of all. H-h-he raped me w-w- w-hen I-I w-was th-th-thirteen. I-i-it was the most painful thing that has ever happened to me. H-h-he took every good part of me that night and ground it to dust. It blew away, mixing with all the other dust. That night, I finally knew what created the dust of Baghdad. It was not made up of dirt but of the crushed hopes, dreams, innocence, and pain of the entire city." I stopped speaking, unable to continue as sobs wracked my body. I stared at the floor the entire time I told my story, not wanting to see Akmal's disappointment, hurt, and disgust. I felt his hands on my face, urging me to look up. Knowing I could not put it off any longer, I hesitantly looked into his eyes.

"My pure, Hanen. I am so sorry you went through that and carried that burden by yourself all these years." He looked into my eyes with just as much love as before, I told him.

"Did you hear anything I said? I am not pure. I did not come to you pure. I was dirty and used up before I even met you!"

"*Habibti*, come here," he pulled me onto his lap, cradling me against his chest like a precious treasure. "You are my pure Hanen. You did nothing wrong, my love."

"Aren't you angry? I lied to you!" I said against his shirt.

"Of course I'm angry. I am furious with Mahki. If I ever see him again, I will not be responsible for what I do to him. That he would hurt you, my beautiful wife, like he did when you were just a child is unforgivable. But Hanen, look at me," he lifted my chin so I could look directly into his beautiful brown eyes, "I am not angry with you. I could never be angry with you. My heart is broken for you; you were abused, and no one was there to protect you. I wish to Allah that I had been there. I would have crushed Mahki like the cockroach he is. I am more in love with you now than before you told me. And I didn't even know it was possible to love you more. You are already my heart. *Habibti*, you are a strong, remarkable, beautiful, pure woman. I am so blessed that Allah sent you to me as a wife."

I searched his eyes, looking for signs that he was hiding his true feelings about what I had done, but all I saw was pure love and acceptance.

For the next hour, I sat with my husband, crying and slowly beginning to heal. If Akmal could love me and see me as pure and beautiful, maybe I could also begin to see myself that way.

Present Day, Office of Dr. Allison Peters

I sat in Allison's office the following Wednesday, excited to tell her about my conversation with Akmal.

"Hello, Hanen. You look happy today. You have a beautiful smile."

"Thank you, Allison. I am happy. I finally told Akmal about what Mahki did to me. I feel like a thousand-pound load stone has been removed from my shoulders." I couldn't stop smiling. Was this how normal people felt all the time? I had no idea. Maybe I would ask Allison about it.

"I take it from your smile that he took the news well?" she asked.

"He took it better than well. He was perfect. He called me his "pure Hanen" even after I told him everything! I couldn't believe he could still stand to look at me, much less consider me pure and beautiful. I was sure he would send me away at the very least, maybe even divorce me. I had made plans for me and my children to stay with my best friend in Canada, Allissa, and her family until I could get my own apartment. I've been saving money since we married, just in case he found out." Until I told Allison all my plans, I didn't realize how much fear I had been living with.

"Hanen, you are a strong and resourceful woman. Most people would crumble under the emotional strain you have lived under. I am so proud of you for telling Akmal. I know that was your greatest fear. You are fighting hard to heal and live a healthy and full life. Most people don't understand how much work it is to undo the damage that years of trauma have done to your psyche. Healing doesn't just happen. It takes dedication, hard work, and vulnerability.'

"I had no idea how much work this would be. But I knew I would go completely crazy if I didn't do something. After my breakdown on my birthday, I could no longer push down all the pain and anger." I stare at the wall, remembering how shattered I had been a few months ago.

"I think your subconscious knew that you were in a safe place to start to deal with your past. I am always amazed at how our brains protect us. In this case, you knew it was time to heal and live a full and complete life, free to be happy and unencumbered by the pain of your past."

"I think you're right. I never thought I deserved to live a happy life. I thought I had sinned too much, was too broken, and tarnished. I was grateful that Allah blessed me with Akmal as a husband. But I never thought he would stand by me and love me if he found out. Now I'm starting to believe I can live a "normal" life with my family. Is that crazy to think?"

"It is not crazy at all. You deserve to live a happy and healthy life. I absolutely believe that you will. Personally, I don't believe that "normal" exists. I think everyone has to deal with something. But you have certainly had to deal with so much more than most people."

"What you say makes sense in my head. But my heart feels differently. I don't know how to forgive myself for this." I say, frustrated by my own limitations.

"This is hard work. Don't get frustrated with yourself. You've been holding onto these secrets for most of your life. It will take time to work through everything."

"I know you're right. But I want to do the work and get to the other side. I don't want to have to deal with this anymore. It has taken up too much of my life. I want to be free of it!" I started to raise my voice. "I'm sorry. I didn't mean to yell."

"First of all, you didn't yell. But if you had, it would have been fine. In fact, I think you should yell if you feel like it. Throw things if you need to, as long as you aren't throwing them at people. Cuss. Do whatever you need to do to let those feelings out. They need to come out, Hanen."

"I think I might end up in the looney bin if I go around screaming, cussing, and throwing things." I give a small chuckle at the thought.

"I'm not suggesting that you stand in the middle of the street in downtown Alberta and throw a fit. But in the privacy of your home, while you are in the shower, or even in the car. I have one client that would go to an amusement park and ride the roller coasters just so they could scream out their pain and frustration. That worked for them. Some people write their feelings. Others paint them. I even had a client that would put on heavy metal music and scream along with it. You need to find a healthy and safe way to release your pain. In fact, that is your assignment for this week. Find a safe way to let your feelings out."

"Why do you keep saying a safe way? Do you think I'm going to do something unsafe," I ask.

"Too often, people find unsafe ways to release their pain. They self-harm, abuse drugs or alcohol, overeat, or starve themselves. I think you know what I'm talking about. I've noticed that your arms are often pink and raw."

"I'm not trying to hurt myself," I say defensively. "I just want to feel clean. I never feel clean. So, I take a lot of hot showers and scrub myself until I feel like I have washed away some of the filth that covers me."

"You know you aren't trying to wash away physical dirt, don't you?" Allison waits for me to answer.

"I know that in my head, but it doesn't feel that way. I feel dirty to my core." I looked at my fingernails, seeing the invisible dirt under them, dirt no one else could see.

"I understand. For now, I will ask you to limit yourself to two ten-minute showers daily. I want you to keep the temperature no hotter than what you wash your children with."

"That is unreasonable. There is no way I can get clean in that amount of time and with water that cool." I push back.

"Hanen, you are hurting yourself. You aren't in a healthy headspace to be able to judge what is normal and not excessive. For now, you need rules to keep you safe. It won't be like this forever. I want you to write every time you shower, how long the shower is, and how hot in your journal and bring it with you next week. When you feel like you will crawl out of your skin if you don't take a hot shower, I want you to practice a healthy way of releasing your pain. It won't feel natural at first. But trust me, this will help you."

"Fine! I'll do it for one week. That is all I will promise," I sulk.

"I appreciate that you are willing to try it. Thank you, Hanen. I'll see you next week."

CHAPTER TWELVE

The Difficult Choice

Sixteen Years Old, Baghdad, Iraq

I tip-toed outside to the tarma, being careful not to wake anyone. I climbed the ladder to the roof and sat on one of the chairs, staring at the night sky.

The sky was filled with stars, their brightness a tapestry of light on a canvas of black. They seemed at once impossibly distant and incredibly close. It seemed to me the longer I stared at them, the more I was drawn toward them and away from Earth. I felt strange, like my body was lifted from Earth and transported through that vast blanket of stars without consent or having any say about where I was going. I could not influence where I was taken or what I experienced. I could only survive it. This feeling of powerlessness was familiar to me, and I began to weep at the futility of it all.

I remembered falling from the roof when I was thirteen years old. Our dog had jumped at me, and I had slipped and tumbled over the edge. I felt the same sense of disconnection then. A few months earlier, the day before Makhi took what was left of my innocence and left me shattered on the bathroom floor, I had felt a similar disassociation when I had snapped the black stick from Makhi's game and been hypnotized by the wriggling black worms that stained the wood.

Ten years ago, when I was six, Makhi kissed me for the first time, and my childhood was unceremoniously stripped from me. From that moment on, I felt dirty, soiled, and used up; an old woman at the age of sixteen instead of the happy, optimistic virtuous teenager the other girls in my class were.

Sitting on the roof that night, I felt different. I couldn't say exactly why. Maybe maturity had finally given me the strength to deny an adult his unholy desires toward me. In contrast, before, I had been a child programmed to believe that I must obey any adult, no matter what their desire.

Whatever the case, I knew it was over with Makhi.

Makhi would just have to accept my decision. I no longer feared his reaction. He had already hurt me in every way he could without killing me. I would not let him continue to abuse me.

It all would come to an end. I knew this as I floated through the universe. I felt the presence of Allah, comforting me as I wept out my pain. A peace settled over me that I hadn't felt since I was six years old. It wasn't complete peace. I still felt soiled and dirty. I doubted anything would ever change that, but at least I was now free to make my own choices, free of abuse and pain. At some point, I drifted into a peaceful sleep, cradled by the moon's light, endless stars, and Allah's love.

"Hana!" I awoke to the sound of my mother's voice. "What are you doing up there?"

I blinked, and the tapestry of stars vanished, replaced by the bright blue of daylight, broken only by the searing yellow-white of the summer sun.

I covered my eyes against the sun's brightness, sat up, and stretched.

"What are you doing, Hana?" my mother called again. "School begins in twenty minutes! You have your final exams soon. You need to get moving so that you aren't late!"

I looked down at my mother, standing at the ladder's base but didn't reply. From the roof, she seemed small and insignificant. I felt a flash of anger as I looked at her. Weak, foolish, vain woman, I thought. Why do you now care about my future when you have cared so little about my present? Your brother has been hurting me for most of my life, and you couldn't be bothered to notice.

My anger with her didn't remove my shame, so I kept my thoughts to myself. Instead, I said, "Don't worry, Mother. As you see, I'm dressed and ready to leave right now. I won't be late for the oh- so-important college entrance exams. However, we already know they will only confirm how precisely average I am and prepare me for my eventual career as an exasperated housewife."

The erudition of this reply contrasted beautifully with my claim of intellectual averageness. My mother's face burned bright red. "If you think you're big enough to disrespect me like that, Hana, you can feel free to come here and prove it."

"If I do that, I'll be late for school," I replied snarkily.

Without waiting for her response, I crawled down the ladder and left for school. My mother glared at me as I walked past but said nothing.

The entrance exams went exactly as expected. I was told I would receive the results in three weeks, but I knew what they would say. I would be accepted into a school but not a great one. I would be accepted into a program but not a great one. I would have a life but not a great one.

A surge of anger ran through me, so powerful it surprised me. Why should I remain here? I had no future in Iraq. I had wanted to escape this dusty, war-torn country for as long as I could remember. My future was lost when Mahki despoiled me, and I stopped caring about anything but surviving. I could either accept life as a housewife, subject to the whims of someone else's desire or escape and build a new life elsewhere.

The reality of my situation hit me almost as fast as the thought of escaping. Where would I go? The nations surrounding Iraq were no better. In fact, some were in worse condition. I couldn't go to America. Iraqis and Muslims, in general, were ostracized and hated by a population that blamed all Muslims for the actions of a few radicalized and unhinged individuals. Europe's hatred of Muslims was even more long-standing than America's. There was nowhere for me to go.

I was stuck.

I was stuck, but I could do something to improve my circumstances. Uncle Makhi was visiting, and I would end ten years of abuse at his hand.

I planned everything I would say—all the accusations, emotions, and anger I would hurl at him when we spoke. I hurried at the thought, suddenly feeling like I would explode if I didn't talk to him immediately. I raced down the streets so fast that it only took me ten minutes to reach home.

I arrived home to find Uncle Makhi in his usual spot on the swing in the tarma. When he saw me, his eyes lit up. He waved and beckoned me over to come sit with him.

Seeing him, my anger faded. After all, wasn't this my fault too? I sat next to him, smiled, and greeted him. "Hi, Uncle Makhi."

"Hello, Hanen! Goodness! Look how big you are!"

It was a silly thing to say to a nearly grown woman, but then, Makhi was never the best conversationalist. I smiled tolerantly and thanked him. Then my smile faded. "Makhi, it's over."

His brow furrowed in confusion. "What's over?"

"It's over, Makhi."

He looked confused for a few seconds longer. Then he understood. "Ah," he said. He fell silent for several awkward moments. Finally, he said. "Yes, you're right. I think that is best."

Maybe he could tell that I meant every word. I had to be sure he understood my feelings. I explained, "It was wrong, Uncle Makhi, what we did. It was always wrong. It was never going to last forever. It was a great sin."

He nodded and looked away. "Yes," he said softly. "It was."

For a moment, I saw in his eyes the same self-loathing that followed me ever since he first touched me. It occurred to me for the first time that he hated himself as much as I hated myself. For that moment, I could feel no anger, only compassion.

How persistently we try to excuse the sins of those we love! How hard we fight to convince ourselves that they are not actually evil but only misguided. We love them, we say to ourselves, so they must be good people. Even good people do evil sometimes. Right?

I recall, years later, after I moved to Canada and married Akmal, but before I became pregnant with Hamsa, we watched a documentary on tv about a serial killer who preyed on women, charming them before luring, murdering, and dismembering them. In the documentary, his mother insisted that he was a good boy. No matter what others said he had done; she was sure he was still good deep in his soul.

Akmal scoffed when he heard that. "Ridiculous! She's delusional. How could she feel that way, knowing what he did? I will love my children with all my heart, but if they turn out like this man, I will disown them immediately! No one will hear me argue for their goodness after they find the bodies in their basement. Insane woman."

I said nothing when he ranted because I understood exactly how that killer's mother felt. It's one thing to recognize evil in a stranger. It's another thing entirely when the face of that evil is one you have loved your entire life.

So, as Makhi stared at the ground and fought with the guilt that consumed him, I offered no condemnation. Instead, I laid my hand over his and said, "We'll find a way through this somehow. You and I have committed a great sin, but Allah is merciful. We will survive."

My flesh crawls, and bile rises in my throat when I now think of how he had manipulated me to believe I had any part of what happened. But at the moment, as Makhi smiled gratefully at me and squeezed my hand, I felt a sense of goodness, as though by my kindness to him, I was demonstrating a deep holiness. I was such a broken and deceived girl. But I had found the strength to end his constant assaults upon me. Looking back, I honor the shattered girl that I was and how she found the strength to be her own hero.

From that moment on, Makhi never touched me again.

CHAPTER THIRTEEN

Forgiveness

Present Day, Alberta, Canada, Our Apartment

"Why didn't my mother or grandmother stop Mahki? They had to have known what was going on! Our house was small, and he wasn't that discreet." I furiously scrubbed a pan as I contemplated my life. I found my mind wandering more and more as to why my family hadn't intervened. As a mother, I was always aware of my children's habits, attitudes, and behaviors. If either of my children displayed the drastic behavior and emotional changes I had as a child, I would be concerned. I would not stop until I knew what was going on with them.

Yet I was a child in a home where three adults lived, adults who loved me, and yet not one of them had noticed anything? I found this hard to believe.

I dried my hands on a dish rag. I could not go on like this anymore. I needed answers; the only way I would get them was to talk to my mother.

It was several hours before my mother woke, so I continued my chores to keep myself busy. Now that I didn't have an irrational fear that Akmal would leave me, I realized the house was, in fact, almost completely spotless. After finishing the morning's dishes and tidying the living room, I had the entire day free.

I took a walk outside. The warmth of the sun wrapped around me like a comforting blanket. I had so much in my life to be thankful for.

And I was truly grateful to Allah for his blessings. But I would never be able to fully embrace the beauty of my new life until I laid the pain and trauma of the past to rest.

I walked toward the park where Akmal and I had gone after my birthday dinner months ago. Though lacking the magical mystery of the stars and the moonlight reflecting off the water, the pleasant brightness of the day held its own charms. I watched as swans and ducks swam, calling each other as they navigated their way to their nests and as songbirds flew from tree to tree, sharing their melodic greetings with the world. Chipmunks darted across the grass between trees to gather acorns for winter though it was still several months away. Such industrious little creatures. People—couples, families, children, and the occasional lone wanderer, meandered down the lazy paths that wound through the park.

The world was busily moving around me. Happiness was a canopy that covered all the park's inhabitants, human and animal alike. Though I was more at peace than I had been since I was six, I still felt separated from the joy that seemed to come so easily to all around me. It was as if I stood within a glass box, a transparent barrier that made me a silent observer of the world, seeing but unable to participate.

When I reached home, determination replaced any nerves I might have felt. I needed answers and was finally ready to confront my mother.

Before I called her, I prayed to Allah for strength and guidance. I thanked Him for His goodness and asked Him for the courage to say what needed to be said.

My phone buzzed. I saw it was a heart-shaped emoji captioned with: "Thinking of you."

My heart fluttered from the romantic gesture. I smiled and replied with a heart emoji of my own. He could not have known how such a seemingly inconsequential gesture would give me the courage to see my mission through. It amazed me how strengthening it was to know that he would always love me and have my back no matter what may come our way.

At last, it was time. I picked up the phone and dialed the number, my heart pounding.

My sister Bayza answered.

"Hana!" she cried out. "Oh, it's so good to talk to you! How have you been?"

We talked for a few minutes, exchanging everything that had happened since we last spoke. After her, I talked to Rabi, then Uncle Ibraham, who was visiting my mother.

"It has been good to talk to you, Uncle Ibraham. Tell your family I said hi and send my love and prayers for Allah's continued blessings upon them." I said, nerves making my voice tight, "Could I speak with Mother?"

A moment later, my mother's voice said, "Hello? Hanen?"

I didn't answer my mother right away. At the sound of her voice, all the memories came flooding back—Makhi's abuse, pain and hurt, mother's emotional distance, helplessness, and loneliness, knowing I could never trust her to help me through my suffering. My strength and resolve began to waver.

"Hello? Hanen, are you there?"

I felt my shoulders lift a little as my strength returned. The anger and hurt had returned, but my confidence was undiminished. I would end this once and for all. Today I would have my answers. As tears welled in my eyes, I finally responded, "Hello, Mother."

"Hana!" Mother answered brightly. "It's so good to hear from you! Oh, I'm so glad you called. How is Akmal?"

"He's fine, Mother. He's at work."

"Of course he is. I'm so glad you found a hardworking man to care for you. And my grandchildren? How are they?"

"They're fine, Mother."

"Growing like weeds and into everything, I'm sure," Mother commented. "I remember when you were young. You were always getting into things, even as a baby. You used to drive me so crazy! It's good that your father was much more patient than I was. I don't know what I would have done to you or your sisters if I was left to my own devices."

"Mother…"

"Wait one moment. I'll go get your father." "No.".

"No? Is everything okay?"

"Everything's fine, Mother. I just need to talk to you alone." There was a pause on the other line. "What's wrong, Hanen?" "Nothing is wrong," I responded, trying to keep the tears out of

my voice. "Not anymore."

"Hanen, you're scaring me. What's wrong? Tell me. You know you can talk to me."

At that statement, my anger welled up inside me until it overflowed. The tears I had held at bay now trickled down my cheeks, and I said, "No, Mother. I couldn't talk to you. That was the problem."

"Yes, you can. You always could." she insisted. "What's happened? Is someone hurt? Is Akmal...."

I ignored her and continued to speak, my voice growing louder as I continued. "I can't talk to you, Mother. I never could. I've never been able to talk to you about anything for forty years because you were emotionally unavailable and preoccupied. My whole life, I've never been able to count on you to listen. You've never shown me compassion. I've always felt judged and alone despite your acts of love."

"Hanen," Mother said, shock and hurt evident. "What has gotten into you? What have I done to you that you are lashing out at me this way?"

"What have you done? What have you done? What haven't you done, Mother? No, don't answer that, I'll tell you. You haven't once told me you were proud of me."

"But I am proud of—"

"You haven't once told me you were there for me if I needed you."

"Hana, I just said—"

"Stop interrupting me!" I was shouting and grateful that I was alone in the house. I hoped our neighbors couldn't hear me, but I didn't dwell on that thought for long. Now that the floodgates were open, every thought I'd kept to myself for years was pouring out, and I couldn't have stopped myself if I wanted to.

"Never, Mother! Never once have I been able to share anything with you! Not my fears. Not my struggles. Not the pain and worthlessness I've felt for as long as I can remember. All those nights, I cried myself to sleep. All those days, I h-hid from the world, from everyone, hoping to disappear because I knew I would find only judgment from the one person who, above all others, should have cared for and protected me."

"Hanen—"

"No, Mother! No! You were never there for me! All you ever did was tell me I wasn't good enough! Not good enough at school! Not well-behaved like Shameera or smart like Bazya. I was a disappointment to you. You told me that much. You made it very clear how much I let you down. You made it clear that every accomplishment of mine was meaningless while every mistake was magnified. You may have said you loved me—if so, I can't remember when—but you clearly never meant it."

"Hanen!" Mother shouted into the phone. "Stop it! Stop it at once!"

Her voice was breathy and high-pitched. I took perverse pleasure in the knowledge that I had rattled her. "Why, Mother? Why stop? Am I letting you down? Is my behavior bringing shame to you?"

"Hanen!" Mother shrieked into the phone. Her voice shook, and I knew she was on the verge of tears, but I felt no sympathy for her.

All of my sympathy for those who had hurt me was gone. "Hanen, tell me what is going on!"

"You want to know what's going on? Makhi abused me, Mother!" I finally shouted. "He abused me! He touched me! For *years*, Mother.

As far back as I can remember that snake of a man touched me and used me and hurt me for his pleasure. He raped me when I was thirteen years old, Mother!"

"Stop that!" Mother spat. "Stop saying that!" Her voice was breathy and ragged. "How can you say that?"

"Because it's true, Mother. Makhi was molesting me in our own home, right under your nose, and you never saw it."

"No," she whispered. "No, no, no, it's not true. It can't be true.

No, no., no—"

"Yes, Mother," I said. "It is. As surely as the sun will set over that bastard's head tonight, it is true. I came to Akmal, a soiled woman, mother. I should have been pure for my husband, but I wasn't. I was a used-up before I even grew into a woman."

"Oh," Mother breathed, and now I could hear her weeping. "Oh no. Oh, Hanen, my baby, I'm so sorry."

"You're sorry? What am I supposed to do with that mother? Will sorry change the years I suffered in silence? Will it make me pure again? Will it punish your brother for abusing me, for raping me? What will your apology do other than allow you to feel better?"

"Hana, I never knew."

"How could you not know? He did it in our small house, which was bursting at the seams with people. How could you be so oblivious to me that you missed how much I changed, my mood swings, my anger? How could you miss my pain? You would have only had to talk to me, to ask, which you never did. Not knowing doesn't excuse you, Mother. It's only proof of your guilt."

"Hanen, I would move Heaven and Earth to take your place. I would never have allowed him to touch you if I knew what was happening."

"You would have known if you'd shown me any attention or any sign that I could talk to you without fear of rejection."

"Hanen, I—I tried. I was hard on you, but only because I loved you."

I laughed bitterly. "Oh, I see. So, you weren't at all jealous, I suppose, of the fact that Grandma was kind to me and protected me."

"No, never. I was never jealous, Hanen. I was worried. Your grandmother wanted you to be a traditional Iraqi woman who cooked, cleaned, and tended the house. She wanted you in the kitchen like a good little girl. I wanted more for you. I only pushed you so hard in school because I wanted you to have a chance at a better life. Look at me, Hanen. I've spent my whole life in a kitchen. I don't know anything better. Your grandmother Khadja never allowed it. Women were to stay home and not concern themselves with the outside world. I was smart and did well in school, Hanen. But I was only allowed to go until the sixth grade! My father made me marry while I was still young. I had no chance to explore and know the world. I wanted better for you!"

"So, you don't want to be with Dad?"

"Of course I do. Your father is a kind and gentle man, and Allah has blessed me with him, but I wanted you kids to have the chance to leave if you could. I wanted so much for you to have control of your life that I never had."

I didn't answer right away. I'd never considered what it must have been like for a smart and talented woman like my mother to live with a woman like my grandmother. I thought about how hard it must have been for my mother to constantly hear all her "failures" pointed out by my grandmother and hold her tongue, never answering back.

Though I sympathized with her, my sympathy wasn't strong enough to dispel my anger. "If Grandma made you feel trapped, Mother, why didn't you do things differently with me? If you hated Grandma so much for not supporting and nurturing you, why didn't you support and nurture me?"

"You weren't like me, Hanen. I fought constantly to have a better life. I may not have succeeded, but I fought hard for it. I never gave up, and when I could no longer fight for myself, I fought for my children: for you and your sisters. I never stopped trying, but you never seemed to try. From an early age, it seemed you gave up. You didn't want to put any effort into bettering yourself. I had to push you. If I hadn't, you'd be stuck here."

"I didn't give up, Mother; I was traumatized from abuse!" "I didn't know that back then."

"Of course you didn't. How could I have talked to you?"

"Hanen, I am sorry. You may never believe me, but I am. I love you. You may never believe me, but I do. You must believe that I did my best to be a good mother. I am not perfect, Hanen. I know now how horrible of a mistake I made with you, and I will never forgive myself. I will never expect you to forgive me, either. I know something of the horrors you experienced because I experienced something similar as a girl. I tried to protect you from experiencing the same pain. Just know that my mistakes were made with the best of intentions. I only ever wanted you to be happy."

I didn't speak for a long time. I weighed what my mother had said. I reflected on her childhood with grandma. I didn't believe my mother was lying. I remembered Grandma Fatima, and she was quite traditional. It made sense that she would forbid her daughters an education as vehemently as my mother demanded it. And it was true that my education allowed me to build a better life for myself. So, in her own misguided way, my mother really had helped me.

And Makhi's abuse wasn't her fault any more than it was mine. Who would suspect their brother of molesting his own niece? I was angry at her, and I couldn't ignore that her harshness with me made it nearly impossible for me to talk to her, but I couldn't blame her for my suffering either.

"Hanen? Are you there?"

"Yes, Mother. I'm here," I said softly.

"Hanen, I'm so sorry." She was weeping now, and her words were barely intelligible over the phone. "I'm so sorry."

"I know, Mother."

My mother only wept in response.

I continued. "I didn't consider that your own mother would have been as hard on you as you were on me. You've suffered, too, and I shouldn't discount that. And you're right. Because I have an education, I was able to build a better life for myself. Thank you. But I will have to work through what happened with Mahki and how you didn't see it. I will try to forgive you, but I am not there yet."

My mother wept for a long time. My own tears were silent, but they streamed down my face continually. Finally, my mother said, "Oh, that snake. Oh, that snake Makhi."

"Yes," I agreed. "That evil snake."

"I'm going to cut his balls off," she said venomously. "I'm going to tell your father, and we're going to castrate the pig for what he did to you."

"No," I said firmly. "Don't tell Dad." As much as the thought of ripping Makhi's balls off appealed to me, I didn't want my father to deal with the inevitable guilt of realizing his daughter was molested right under his nose. He had worked so hard to provide for us during those war-torn years when food was as much a luxury as a necessity. He did not need to burden himself for not being there when he had worked himself to the bone so we could eat. I also worried about how he would react to the shame of what had happened to me. Many girls in Iraq were killed by their families because of the shame that losing their purity brought upon the family. This was not in the Quran. Allah loves all his daughters, especially those hurt and abused. But people are imperfect creatures and have twisted Allah's will that we are pure before him, meaning that women should be killed for abuse they had no control over.

My father is a kind and gentle man. He would never blame me, but I did not want to humiliate him or our family.

"Oh, Hana," my mother wept. "Oh, I'm so sorry. If only I had known," she lamented. "I could have helped you."

"But you didn't know," I said. "I understand why you thought you had to be so hard on me. And I am glad you pushed me to finish school."

We wept together over the phone, and when we were done weeping, we talked for a long time. I shared the news of Akmal and talked about Hamsa and Hamid. She gossiped about my sisters and Dad's job. I asked how Grandma Khadja was doing. "Well, age is hard on everyone, but she's alert and healthy enough to drive me crazy, so that's a good sign," she laughed.

"That's good," I replied. "I need to come visit you soon."

A few minutes later, I hung up with a promise to arrange a visit before the year was out.

Talking to my mother felt like a huge weight lifted off my shoulders, but I still felt angry. I tried to remember the good times throughout my childhood, but all I could remember was the pain and hurt. It was an unwanted movie that replayed itself on the screen of my mind in full technicolor while the rest of my childhood was shown in muted black and white.

Present Day, the office of Dr. Allison Peters

I sat silently on the overstuffed leather couch in Allison's office, waiting for her to join me. I thought back to all those months ago when I had first arrived. I was a broken, angry, defeated woman who blamed herself for all that had happened.

But look at me now! I was healing. I no longer hid who I was and what I had experienced. And people still loved me. I knew my worth before Allah and my husband. I was finally beginning to dream again. I'd even enrolled in classes!

I was thankful that Sama had insisted I start therapy because I don't think I would have made as much progress without Allison's direction. She had made such a difference in my life. I hoped today would be no different because I faced another challenge in my healing journey.

"Good morning, Hanen. How have you been since we last met?"

"Good morning. I have been doing well. I kept track of my showers in my journal, as you asked. Did you want to see it?"

"No, that is your personal journal. Just tell me how it went. How did you feel not taking the long, super-hot showers?"

"Honestly, it was hard. I never thought about it, but I've used showers to cope since I was little. I never looked at it as self-harming. I felt the overwhelming need to wash myself clean of Makhi and his disgusting hands. The showers became progressively hotter and longer the more that Mahki did to me. Eventually, the water wasn't enough, and I had to scrub him off my skin. I scrubbed harder and harder. It was never enough." I paused, wanting to gather my thoughts. "This week, every time I wanted to take a long, hot shower and scrub myself clean, I had to really think about what was happening and deal with it because the shower was no longer an option. I'm not going to tell you that I don't have the desire to do it anymore, but I am beginning to see a pattern. I want to hurt myself when angry, stressed, or hurt. Instead of dealing with the person who hurt me or made me mad, I hurt myself." I shrugged, a little embarrassed by the admission.

"Hanen, you are making so much progress. And you are doing it so quickly. It is very apparent how dedicated you are to healing. Keep doing what you are doing. And one day, you will wake up and realize the past doesn't have quite the hold on you that it once did. That isn't to say you won't have scars or things that trigger you. Because anyone who survives trauma carries their fair share of scars. But you will find that you can acknowledge and move past that pain. Your life will revolve around the present and what you enjoy." Allison smiled at me and reached over to squeeze my hand, a habit of hers that I had noticed early on.

"I did have something happen this week that I wanted to talk with you about," I looked at her, waiting for her response.

"Of course, tell me what is on your mind."

"One of the things that I figured out when I stopped self-harming is that I am angry with my family, especially my mother, for not protecting me when I was a girl. I had so many questions, so I called and confronted her with the truth of what had happened to me. I found out that she was assaulted throughout her childhood. She also explained why she was so hard on me as a girl." I grab a chocolate kiss from the dish she has sitting on the table next to the couch, unwrap it, and pop it into my mouth. The sweet chocolate melting on my tongue gave me time to organize my thoughts.

"Wow, that sounds like an intense conversation. How do you feel now that you got everything out into the open?"

"Honestly, I'm even more angry now. I know I should feel compassion for all she has been through. She experienced more trauma than even I did. But instead, I find myself more baffled that she did not notice what was happening and did not stop it. Having experienced it herself, she had to know!" I felt the anger again creeping up from my core, a burning rage that felt like it had a life of its own. "And I feel ashamed for being angry. She is a good woman who did her best to show us her love. She would take any scrap of fabric she could find to sew clothes for our dolls. And she would paint beautiful murals on our walls so that our home was a place of beauty amidst the rubble of Baghdad. She is talented and smart. I know I should forgive her...." my voice trailed off.

"First, your feelings aren't wrong or right. They are your emotions. To assign them a moral weight is to give them more power than they have. It isn't wrong of you to be angry. In fact, it is understandable. As a child, the adults surrounding you were supposed to protect you, but they didn't. Denying or trying to suppress how you feel won't change it. You'll just add a layer of guilt over top of those feelings you'll have to work through too." Allison took a sip from a coffee mug that read, *"I shrink; therefore, I am."*

"I suppose you're right. But I also know that Allah blesses those who forgive." I sighed, frustrated that my faith and emotions were not more aligned.

"I'm not saying that you shouldn't forgive your mother. But before you forgive, you must work through your anger and hurt. Otherwise, you aren't forgiving. You are just suppressing your emotions. As a child, you learned to suppress and ignore your emotions to survive the abuse you endured. It was a necessary defense mechanism at that time. But now, it is your first instinct to suppress your feelings. But you can only push them down for so long before they find other, usually unhealthy, ways to come out."

"So how do I "work through" my anger, hurt, and resentment? It seems like an impossible task. The more I think about my childhood, the angrier I get!" The red-hot rage was trying to crawl up from my belly where it seemed to live, always roiling and clawing to get out. I was afraid if it ever did, it would consume me and everyone around me.

"I wish I could give you a magic pill, and poof," Allison made a gesture like my fairy godmother granting my wishes with a wand, "you could suddenly forgive, but that pill doesn't exist. Instead, forgiveness is another step in your healing that takes time and a lot of work."

"Ugh, I was afraid you were going to say that." I give a half-groan and rub my temples.

"Let's put that down and come back to it another day. It's okay to need time to process," she gave me a small smile.

"Yeah, I don't think I'm ready to dig into all that today. But how could she miss what happened to me when she experienced it herself? I mean, my parents were very overprotective. We couldn't spend the night at friends' houses. We couldn't play with the other children in the neighborhood beyond 5 or 6 pm. My mother always told us to stay alert and be safe. My parents' overprotectiveness made my sisters and I distrust everyone we met. To be honest, most people in Iraq don't trust anyone. You never know when your neighbor may lie and say that someone in your house is a terrorist for the reward. They aren't evil at heart, but hunger can make the purest heart do the unthinkable." I could hear how empty and hard my voice sounded. But unless a person had experienced what the horrors of war did to a nation, there was no way that they could understand.

"The trauma that you, your family, and your country have experienced is something else we must discuss. But for today, I will focus on the first part of your question, how could your mother miss what was happening to you when she experienced the same thing?" Allison paused, taking another sip from her mug. "This is not as unusual as you might think. People who have been abused often miss the abuse happening to others around them. This is due to a combination of issues. The first is "normalization." Normalization is when abuse victims see harmful behaviors as standard because their view of "normal" has been distorted, making it hard to identify abusive behaviors or red flags.

Abuse victims often experience dissociation and denial as a way to protect themselves. Seeing the signs of abuse can trigger them, bringing back memories of their own trauma.

Desensitization goes along with normalization and dissociation. Desensitization is when an abused victim shuts down and is emotionally numb. This defense mechanism protects them from the trauma they have experienced. But it can make them oblivious to the emotional state of others as well.

Lack of education is another big reason people miss the signs of abuse. Just because someone is abused does not mean they have been taught the signs and behaviors to look for to identify possible abuse victims around them.

Guilt and fear can cause victims to ignore the abuse signs around them. They might see signs of abuse but are afraid to acknowledge or intervene due to fear of retaliation or a misplaced sense of guilt. They might believe recognizing and intervening in abusive situations might make things worse."

"Hearing all this makes me afraid that I will miss the signs. What signs should I look for to protect my children and others?" I shook my head, the thought of anyone hurting my children making me want to scream and vomit simultaneously.

"The signs can vary depending on the situation and individuals. Also, these things are not definitive. It is important to remember that they can be but aren't always indicative of abuse. But here are some common signs to look for in children.

Changes in behavior, if a child has a sudden and extreme change in behaviors, such as being a laid-back child and suddenly they are always angry, or they used to talk a lot and suddenly stop talking. These changes can be signs that they are being abused.

Children often struggle academically when there is abuse happening. It is particularly significant if a child has not had academic struggles. Then suddenly, their grades start dropping without an identifiable cause.

A child may also regress when experiencing abuse. Regression is when a child loses skills that they have already mastered. For example, they may start bed-wetting, stop talking, or begin to suck their thumb again.

Several other indicators are poor hygiene, difficulty sleeping, complaining about their genitals itching or hurting, the inability to sit in a chair without pain, fear of specific people or places, frequent absences from school, and unexplained injuries.

"That is a lot to process. It all makes sense, but it is overwhelming." I rubbed my temples again, the headache behind my eyes worsening.

"We have covered a lot. Let's stop for today. This week, take some time to digest everything we discussed. Then make a list of signs of your abuse that your parents missed. Take your time. If you feel overwhelmed or upset, put the list down for a while and return to it when you feel emotionally ready. Remember, healing is a marathon, not a sprint. Your abuse didn't happen overnight; your healing will also take time."

CHAPTER FOURTEEN

Seven Times YES!

19 years old, Baghdad Iraq

Dad turned the key, and the engine turned over but didn't start. He turned the key again with the same result.

"Come on," he muttered. He turned the key again, and this time the engine sputtered a couple of times, then roared to life.

"Yes!" he cried, slapping the steering wheel in victory. He turned to me and grinned. "You see? I told you she would run."

"That you did," I said, returning his smile. The truth was, I was relieved because walking to University was very dangerous. The rioting and looting had quieted down considerably, but it wasn't yet unheard of for people to be mugged on their way to work or school. The car offered a small measure of safety.

My father pulled out gently and drove slowly, eyes flicking over the road. His anxiety was written in every line of his face, and his smile now seemed almost ill rather than happy. My own smile faded as I remembered the reason for his fear.

Though the fighting had stopped months ago, the danger had not passed. The ground was littered with spent shell casings, and much of the rubble from the destroyed buildings remained exactly where it had fallen. Bombs and mines lay buried throughout the city. The police force—what was left of it, at least—claimed to have removed most of them but last week alone, there were two explosions caused inadvertently by drivers rolling over a mine.

When the fighting stopped, we expected the Americans to remain in the city and deter any further uprising with military presence. Unfortunately, public opinion in America finally became vocal enough against the war that the American president decided to reduce the American presence in Iraq. This meant the soldiers left, and they no longer needed to clean up their mess. Why did it matter if a few warheads were left behind? They weren't staying.

So, the Baghdad Police were left to do their best. Within a week, three warheads detonated, killing over thirty officers. After that, the police abandoned the job, and we citizens were essentially left to our own devices. From one perspective, we were lucky. Only five warheads had detonated in the four months since the Americans left, and only sixty-seven people died. Other cities had suffered much worse.

Knowing that others had suffered more did nothing, of course, to ease our suffering. Life was hard enough, even without the constant fear of death. The shelling had contaminated the water supply, so it was no longer fit to drink and had to be filtered and boiled repeatedly. Even then, failure to disinfect it well enough led to devastating illness— diarrhea, dysentery, and vomiting so severe it could, and often did, kill the weaker members of our community.

The winter months proved especially harsh. The resurgence in fighting meant the Americans confiscated most of the oil supply, leaving very little for us to power our stoves, heaters, and cars. The government—which usually provided enough for the entire winter— could now provide only two weeks' worth of oil. The rest we had to buy at outrageous prices. Most people in the city could not afford it.

Many who survived the dirty water succumbed to the cold. They didn't bother to count how many people died of the cold and diseases such as pneumonia and influenza. Still, we all noticed the dwindling numbers of students at school.

My family was one of the lucky ones. Dad's job still paid him well enough to afford oil, so we had enough to heat our home through the winter and cook at least one hot meal daily. We could even put gas in the car, although we could not drive it often.

We had enough for oil and food and almost nothing else. Before the fighting reached us, my father often bought us snacks like chocolates, chips, and ice cream. When we were old enough to trust us to go out alone, he would give us money to enjoy ourselves. After the fighting, we just couldn't afford that anymore. Still, any time my father did have extra money, even if it was only a little, he would give it to us. Once, when we were out, I felt too tired to walk home, and he gave me money for the bus. I accepted gratefully, not realizing he had enough for only one passenger until I boarded the bus, and he remained behind. I called for him to wait, and I would walk home with him, but he urged me on the bus, smiling and begging me not to worry. He could use the exercise, he told me, smiling.

I never considered us to be wealthy. We weren't, not in the academic sense. I realize now that we were far better off than many neighbors. We had barely enough for necessities, but many others didn't even have enough for that. We were fortunate, indeed.

I also appreciated how much my father loved us. I knew he loved us, but I never fully understood our importance to him. When he gave me the last of his bus money and dared the journey home alone, risking mugging and robbery, I realized suddenly that he would lay down his life for me if he needed to. Not until my children were born did I understand the fierce love a parent feels for them.

I reached over and squeezed his hand as he drove. He risked a brief glance at me and smiled. I returned his smile and said, "I love you, Dad."

"I love you too, Hana."

I tilted his hand to stare at his beauty mark—a large, black spot on the back of his right hand. I smiled and closed my palm over it, pressing hard. I wanted a part of it to rub off on me so I could always have a piece of my father with me. I don't think I ever loved him more than I did then.

"If you keep squeezing my hand like that, you'll crush it," he teased.

I relaxed my grip and grinned at him. A memory crossed my mind, and I asked, "Dad, whatever happened to that truck you found last week? The one with all of the oil."

"Oh, that. I had my employees dispose of it."

I stared in shock. "Dispose? You mean you threw it away?" "Yes. That was the best solution."

"To throw it away? Dad, people are dying! We could have helped so many poor people with that oil!"

"It wasn't mine to give, Hanen."

"So? Would Allah not forgive you if you used it to help the sick and dying?"

"No, He would not. Allah rewards hard work and humility, not theft, no matter how well-meaning the theft is. This would be stealing from the government. It is haram, forbidden."

"But so many people…"

"Hanen, what would happen if I took that oil? If people found out I had a truckful of oil, we would be attacked and robbed before the day was out."

"Not if you distributed it fairly."

"And what if I did? A truckful of oil could supply three or maybe four hundred people a month. Maybe six weeks if they were frugal, but what happens after that? Who do you think those people will come to when they run out? What of the several hundred thousand others who will still have nothing?"

My father was not angry as he said this, merely mournful. "And when they didn't find any more oil—"

"They would take everything we had and leave us to freeze and starve," he said.

I was filled with anger then. "Why are people so cruel?" I asked. "They're not cruel, Hanen. They're only frightened and hungry.

A desperate person will commit acts even an evil person would abhor,

but we mustn't blame them for it." Still, I felt anger for everything happening around us and the people who invaded and caused so much pain.

Misunderstanding my expression, Dad smiled and ruffled my hijab. "Don't worry too much about it, Hanen. The war is over for us. We will suffer a little while we rebuild, but we will rebuild. This is only another trial. Nothing more."

I couldn't tell my father the real reason for my anger, so I only nodded, forced a smile, and agreed to let it go. We reached school a few minutes later. I said goodbye and walked to class.

Sama met me at the top of the steps. We grinned and embraced each other like long-lost friends. We always greeted each other this way, even though we saw each other daily.

"Hello, sister!" she said brightly. "Hello, brother!" I teased.

She slapped my arm playfully. "If anyone's the brother in this friendship, it's you." She squeezed my bicep. "Look at these arms. I'll bet you can crack walnuts with your bare hands, right?"

"No!" I protested, blushing. "Stop teasing me just because you're the runt of your litter!"

She gasped and lifted her hand to her chest in shock. "Hanen, such mean things you say!"

We laughed and joked that way all the way to the classroom.

It's worth mentioning that I am unusually strong for a girl. I inherited my strength from my mother, who inherited it from Grandmother Huda. Growing up, I was known as the girl with the strength of a boy. This spared me from being targeted by bullies, although it didn't stop Uncle Makhi's abuse. In college, I was still known for my strength and athleticism. I would often impress my classmates by demonstrating my strength. Once, I lifted our teacher's office chair over my head. It was an upholstered metal office chair with an adjustable lift and weighed over fifty pounds. I was proud of my strength, especially because I was not a large girl, so my size didn't give me strength.

A couple of boys waited just outside the classroom. They catcalled us as we approached. "Hello, beauties," one of them said, grinning. "You look like you need husbands."

"Thank you," Sama said sarcastically, "But we'd prefer to marry men."

Several other classmates were watching this interaction, and at Sama's jibe, they oohed and ahhed. The offending boy reddened with embarrassment and tried to save face by turning to his friend and saying, "I'll take the little one. She looks like she needs to learn manners. You can have to big one."

I smiled sweetly at him and approached, swaying my hips a little. His brow furrowed in confusion. I'm sure he'd expected me to be angry. When I was close enough to reach him, I lunged forward and pulled him away from the door. As he stumbled away, I pulled Sama inside and shut the door.

The boys pounded and pushed on the door, but I planted my feet and pressed my shoulder into the door.

"What the hell?" One of the boys exclaimed when he couldn't open it. He and his friend pushed hard, so I had to strain to keep the door closed, but I managed to keep them outside. The other students laughed and cheered, teasing him.

"Come on, Hasim, you can't even open a door held by a girl?"

"Stop helping her!" Hasim cried from the other side.

Of course, no one was helping me, so the other students laughed harder.

This enraged Hasim, and he and his friend threw themselves at the door with all their might. It budged only a few inches before slamming shut again. They continued for a few minutes before I heard our instructor's voice from outside the door. "Hey! What are you two doing? What's going on in there?"

"Hanen won't let us inside!" Hasim whined. "Hanen? The girl, Hanen?"

"She's a freak!" Hasim whined, as Sama and I stifled our giggles. "She's like a gorilla!"

"Well, maybe you shouldn't provoke her if she's so much stronger than you," Professor Sayid quipped.

"She's not—" Hasim began before falling silent.

It was too late. Professor Sayid said, "It seems she is if she managed to hold the door against both of you. Maybe you'd like to say something to her inside and see how it goes for you?"

The boys muttered no, and Professor Sayid knocked on the door. "Hanen? I have two contrite young men and a very tired professor who would like to be allowed into the classroom. May we come in?"

"You may," I said through my laughter. I backed away from the door, and a moment later, an amused Professor Sayid and two red-faced boys entered.

"Thank you," Professor Sayid said politely. "Now, if you all would take your seats, I shall try to make class at least half as interesting as Hanen's victory."

The class laughed again, and Hasim and his friend sank into their chairs. It wasn't long after this that Sama left University to be married in another city. With her departure, my world lost one of its few bright spots.

I leaned back in my chair and tried not to let my boredom show as Professor Sayid lectured. It wasn't that the class was especially boring or that Professor Sayid was a poor lecturer. It's just that the days seemed to drag on with Sama gone. I was still keeping up with my studies—I had to if I ever wanted to leave Iraq and make a life of my own—but it was through sheer force of will and not the enjoyment of learning that I avoided falling behind. With Sama, it was easy. Learning was fun, and studying with her was something I looked forward to. Without Sama, it was tedious.

My malaise didn't disappear at the end of class. Everything about University seemed to have lost its color without my friend who had moved away. I still ate falafel with Pepsi for lunch, sometimes even with other students. Still, whether alone or with other friends, I felt lonely.

The best parts of my day were the drives to and from University with my father and Bayza when we would laugh, joke, and talk. I feared that including Bayza in my time with Dad would mean losing something precious that was just ours, but it was even more fun with her. Like me, Bayza had outgrown much of her immaturity, so we could laugh and talk on an even footing without any sibling rivalry. I appreciated the chance to connect with her. Bayza and I didn't always get along growing up, but the times we did were the brightest parts of a childhood that was too often shrouded in darkness.

Sitting on the steps in front of the campus, waiting for my father and Bayza to pick me up, I realized it had been months since I thought about Uncle Makhi. He still visited occasionally, but apart from the obligatory polite greetings, he and I didn't communicate. He spent a good deal of time with Bayza still. This alarmed me initially, but it was clear very quickly that his interest in her was not like his interest in me, so I let it go.

I tried to push these thoughts away, but now that they had resurfaced, I couldn't stop thinking about them.

Why me? Why only me? Shameera was older than me, but he never showed interest in her. Bayza developed sooner than me, though I developed much faster when I finally began. They were even close with each other like he and I were, yet he never tried anything with her. Rabi, likewise, never received anything but familial attention from Uncle Makhi.

Why only me? What about me made him desire more than the relationship between uncle and niece? Could he tell that he could manipulate and intimidate me into silence?

These thoughts soured an already melancholy mood, so with great shock, I looked up to see the most handsome boy I'd ever seen and felt my memories flee like the night before the rising sun.

He was not exceptionally tall but carried himself in a way that commanded attention. He had chiseled features, and though he wore the modest clothing all Muslims wore regardless of gender, it was clear his body was fit and attractive. His hair was dark and soft and hung gently over his face.

It was his eyes that transfixed me. They were a deep green and seemed to pierce through me like twin daggers, frightening and hypnotizing in their power.

He approached me, smiling, and spoke with a voice that carried the same power as his appearance.

"Good afternoon," he said. "I am Ali. May I sit with you?"

I was too stunned to speak, so I only nodded. Ali sat beside me, a respectable distance away but close enough my heart began to beat rapidly in my chest. Goodness, was this what falling in love felt like? It felt like any second, I would die of a heart attack!

His smile widened slightly, and I suspect he could sense my attraction to him. "Well?" he asked.

"Well, what?" I replied.

"I've told you my name. Now you should tell me yours."

Miraculously, enough of my faculties returned. Rather than simply tittering and melting like a fool, I kept my voice dignified and said, "Oh, and why is that? I've only just met you, after all."

Surprisingly, my sarcasm didn't seem to put him off like it did other boys. He laughed and said, "Well, if you don't tell me your name, I'll have to think of something else to call you."

"Hmm, and what would you like to call me?"

He crossed his arms and reflected, then answered, "Saarah." "Saarah? What made you decide on that?"

"You look like a princess," he said.

Warmth spread through me from head to toe, and the grin on Ali's face told me the flush in my cheeks was clearly visible. I was rescued from further embarrassment by Bayza.

"Hana!" she called. "Are you going to make us wait all day?" I looked down to see Bayza and Dad waiting in the car. "Hana," Ali said. "Well, that's a pretty name, too."

"It's Hanen, actually," I said. "Hana is for short." My face heated again. "I don't know why I said that."

"Hanen," he said. "It's nice to meet you, Hanen."

"Hana!" Bayza called again.

"Well, I shouldn't keep them waiting," I said.

"Of course," he replied. He stood. "I'll see you tomorrow?" "It's a big campus," I replied impudently.

He only smiled softly and replied. "I'll see you again."

In the car, Dad asked, "Who was that boy you were talking to?" His tone was light, but I could sense the anxiety behind it. Apparently, my attraction was noticeable to more than just Ali.

"It's no one," I said. "Just a boy from class."

"He seemed very friendly for a boy from class," Dad replied. "Oh? Well, he's single, I believe. I'll tell him you're interested."

I smiled, expecting him to roll his eyes or scold me playfully, but he only smiled and said nothing.

He was *really* worried about Ali. I found his anxiety amusing but didn't tease him about it. My thoughts were too wrapped up in the boy with green eyes and a gently commanding voice.

***

I smiled at the tiny shrubs with even more minute white flowers lining the walk to the Agricultural Sciences Building. The plants were hardy and common to the deserts of Iraq. They required very little effort to cultivate and grow. Normally, it would not be a particularly impressive showing for a university known for its Agricultural Science program. However, after the destruction of the previous year's fighting, the tiny white blooms were like bright stars of hope.

Things were getting better. It was months now since a bomb had gone off, and the once-cautious government was well into a far more successful second cleanup campaign. The rioting, looting, and mugging had almost stopped completely, and we no longer walked or drove our streets in fear. As with most tragedies, the people of Baghdad came out of it stronger and prepared to return to the calm, peaceful life we valued so much.

I turned to Ali, who smiled at me with his intoxicating smile, "They're beautiful, aren't they? But they pale in comparison to you."

I rolled my eyes but still blushed and grinned at his compliment. "Are you always so imaginative?"

"Should a man not be grateful for the gifts Allah has given him?" I scoffed. "I don't belong to you."

"Not yet," he agreed, "But soon you shall be my very own Rose of Jericho—the brightest jewel in my crown."

"Your crown?" I said, chuckling. "All hail Prince Ali, Sultan of Barley."

"Laugh while you can," he said. "When you are my wife, you will not be permitted to disrespect me like that." He smiled, but there was the slightest edge to his voice, and though I continued to laugh and tease, the alarm in the back of my head sounded once more.

I'd known Ali for four months now, and as the second year of my University education neared its close, I thought more and more of a future with him. I don't know that I could say I loved him. I liked and was attracted to him, but something about him concerned me enough that I couldn't quite give my heart to him.

Every so often, he would say things like this—calling me his flower, his jewel, warning me that when I was his wife, he would make me behave better. Once, I caught him telling his friends he believed I would make an excellent wife because I was strong and should have no trouble keeping a clean house and cooking for him.

He was affectionate and kind to me, and I believe he genuinely liked me. Still, I couldn't always ignore the evidence that he saw me as a prize to be won—a valuable piece of property to possess rather than a partner to be loved and respected.

He was so gentle and generous that I could usually ignore these concerns. Still, he would say something like this every so often, and alarm bells would go off in my head.

Looking back, I know I would never have settled for a marriage with Ali. Of course, I have Akmal, but even if I never met my Amiri, I couldn't have been happy marrying someone who saw me beneath them. It wasn't just me. Like many men, Ali seemed to see all women as existing only for the pleasure and happiness of men.

I only entertained these hopes as long as I did because my feelings for him were the first I could describe as truly romantic. I had one other near-marriage purely motivated by a desire to escape Iraq. There had been no love or romance, just a desperate need to flee the country of my birth. Once my father learned of my long-distance "relationship," it was over and done. Truthfully, I was secretly grateful that he intervened. Obviously, I never felt anything for Makhi that even approached romance. It felt good to feel like I had found normal love, good enough that I was able to ignore the warning signs.

But not forever. The break between my second and third years of University gave me time to reflect. When Bayza sat with me and gently explained that she thought giving up my infatuation with Ali would be best, I didn't protest. She explained that our parents would never approve of a marriage to a farmer, regardless of his success. She explained that it was a hard life, harder than my parents wanted for us.

I nodded and didn't press further. I didn't confront my parents either. I knew the real reason for their reticence had nothing to do with his station in life and everything to do with his treatment of me. So, although I was saddened by the end of my first romance, I was also relieved to know that the temptation was no longer there to settle for the wrong man to escape my life at home.

After the break, we didn't speak. To his credit, he never once disparaged or disrespected me for the end of our association—in private or public. I saw him several times after that, but we never spoke again. Years later, I looked him up out of curiosity. He married another of our classmates and had three daughters with her. I couldn't find much information about him on his social media. Still, the confidence in his wife's eyes and the happiness in his daughters' eyes suggest he learned the proper way to treat women. I wish him well.

***

And so, I entered my third year of University as lonely as I had entered the first and second years. Once again, however, my loneliness was destined to be temporary. I told my parents during the break that I would agree to an arranged marriage. I wasn't entirely excited about the thought, but after two failed attempts at romance, I was ready to allow Allah to guide my choice rather than my deceitful heart. I had little hope of success, at least not for a while, but once more, Allah's grace would shine on me.

One evening my cousins from my father's side visited. One cousin, Tahira, brought a friend to meet my parents--Akmal. She was married and carrying her second child, so there was no suggestion of impropriety. Besides, Akmal was her husband's friend from school and only came along because her husband didn't want her driving in her pregnant state.

In any case, I saw Akmal for the first time and immediately knew he was the man I would marry.

It sounds silly to come out and say it like that, like another frivolous schoolgirl fantasy. Still, as soon as I saw his kind eyes and awkward smile, I knew we would be together. Even before Tahira introduced us and the conversation between him, myself, and my parents made it clear they saw him as a potential husband, I knew we would be with each other.

It's a curious thing, falling in love. Before I met Akmal, I imagined falling in love as an adventure. I was a princess waiting in her tower for the noble knight to woo her by riding his steed on quests of glory and greatness. All to prove his worth before finally sweeping me off my feet and carrying me to a castle in the clouds.

Falling in love with Akmal was nothing like that. He did sweep me off my feet, but the conclusion was long foregone by the time we reached the point of romance. Falling in love with him was like putting on a warm coat or a comfortable pair of shoes. It didn't feel like an adventure. It felt like coming home. I didn't imagine him performing daring feats of glory to win my hand. I imagined walking with him and talking about the most trivial things, sitting together in our home, content to be in each other's presence, squabbling—yes, squabbling! —over household decisions like which appliances to buy or what school to send the children to. I imagined a mundane, boring, simple life that would be anything but mundane or boring with him.

We hit it off right away and spent the evening talking. I learned he was from Canada and worked in retail in Edmonton.

We corresponded throughout my third year of University. He was very sweet and gentle in his communications. Though some of them were as cheesy and foolish as Ali's flirtations, and others were annoyingly condescending—he was thirteen years older than me and in his mid-thirties already when we met—they were sincere and heartfelt. Fifteen years later, he is still the most sincere and genuinely kind person I've ever met. That, above all, is why I love him. That, and he's the most adorably awkward person who's ever lived, of course.

Our courtship continued through my fourth year of university. When my parents called me to speak with them, the conversation—and its resolution—was merely a formality.

"Hanen," my father began, "It's time to discuss your marriage." "To Akmal?" I asked.

He frowned. "To Akmal? Of course not. What are you talking about?

I rolled my eyes as Mom and Dad erupted into peals of laughter. "Ha ha ha," I said. "You're both very clever."

When their laughter subsided, Dad said, "We're very proud of you, your mother, and me. I want you to know that. And I want you to know we understand."

"You understand what?" "Why you need to leave."

"Oh," I replied, shifting awkwardly.

"Iraq is a hard place for a strong, spirited girl like you," Mom explained. "We will miss you terribly. However, in Canada, you will be free to show your strength, and Akmal seems the perfect man to encourage that side of you rather than try to stamp it out."

The briefest ember of anger flashed in me as I wondered why, if Mom felt the way she did, she spent so much of my youth trying to stamp it out herself. It faded as quickly as it arrived, and I embraced them as we wept and celebrated my marriage-to-be.

***

I inhaled deeply and held my breath for several seconds before letting it out slowly. I breathed this way for several minutes, but it did nothing to ease my anxiety.

"Why are you so nervous?" Bayza asked, laughing. "It's not as though you're being sold into slavery."

"I'm not nervous!" I protested in a tone that made it obvious that I was, in fact, incredibly nervous. Today Akmal's mother was coming to our home to meet me and decide if she approved of my marriage to her son.

Akmal had corresponded for nearly two years, and our families knew we would probably marry. But today's visit was the official mother of the groom visit. If she decided that she did not like something about me, the marriage would be off.

I looked in the mirror, checking my makeup and hair for what felt like the hundredth time. I turned from side to side, ensuring my chosen dress showed my figure in the best light. Akmal would not see me without my hijab until the wedding day. It was his mother's job to ensure he would find me attractive. So, she would meet with me without my hijab. I felt excited and nervous as I walked out of my room and sat in our sitting room, waiting for the visit. My mother rushed about like a busy bumble bee flitting from flower to flower, collecting pollen. She double-checked that the sweets and tea were ready to serve. We wanted to make a good impression, showing her the best hospitality.

Akmal's mother arrived promptly at one pm. Traditional visiting hours for these meetings were between 12 – 6. We needed to fulfill all the traditions to have a blessed union between our families and Akmal and me.

I immediately liked her. She was kind and gracious and immediately made me feel more at ease.

"Hanen, you look beautiful. I am excited to have this meeting.

My son has only the most wonderful things to say about you."

I continued to serve the tea, filling the Istikan to the very top before handing it to her as the guest of honor. Once tea was served, I left my mother and Akmal's mother to complete the rest of the meeting without me. Although it was our marriage, Akmal and I had very little to do with the agreements to be reached before we would marry.

There would be more meetings like this between our fathers or our mothers to determine everything from the Nishan that Akmal's family would pay to where we would live after marriage. Would we live in his parents' home, a separate house on their property, or our own place? What food would be served at the Mashaya? Endless details had to be planned in painstaking specificity.

My sisters sat with me in our room the day before my wedding. We were reminiscing about our childhoods and teasing each other as sisters do.

I was sitting in front of the mirror,

"So, you *are* nervous?" Bayza asked, noticing the look on my face. "When you are less than a day away from your marriage, you'll

see how nervous you'll get."

"Not me," Bayza said. "When I marry, my husband will be nervous, not me."

"When you marry, your husband will weep with grief at the unfortunate life that led him to such a sorry state," Rabi quipped.

Rather than responding, Bayza touched Rabi's face with the tip of her henna brush, leaving a small mark on her cheek. Rabi pulled away and cried out while Bayza burst into laughter. I also started to laugh, but we all fell silent when Mom walked in and barked. "You two! Enough playing! Your sister is to be married tomorrow! Act like adults for once and finish her henna!"

"Sorry, Mom," Bayza choked out through laughter.

Rabi rubbed her cheek ruefully and said, "You better hope this comes out by tomorrow, Bayza."

"Oh, quit being dramatic. You'll be fine."

The closer my wedding approached, the more shame I felt. That wasn't the only thing I felt, or even the most dominant feeling. The love I felt for Akmal, the joy for our union, and the anticipation of our life together in Canada quite overpowered the trepidation I felt at the physical consummation of our marriage, but it didn't completely dispel it.

I wasn't pure.

Akmal had taken to calling me that of late. "My pure Hanen." I wasn't pure. I was soiled. I was a fornicator. I was Uncle Makhi's old plaything. Though we hadn't done anything in six years, hearing Akmal call me pure made me feel as dirty and used as though Makhi had just finished defiling me.

Uncle Makhi and the rest of my family would be at my wedding tomorrow. I hated that. I could imagine nothing worse than hearing him congratulate me and seeing him shake Akmal's hand, knowing what he'd done.

I felt suddenly ill and had to sit and put my hands between my knees to prevent myself from vomiting.

"Hanen!" Bayza cried. "My goodness, you really are nervous!" "Of course she is!" Rabi cried. "She's getting married!"

"Hush, Rabi," Bayza said. "Hana, are you okay? Do you need water?"

I shook my head and kept breathing in the same controlled manner. "I'll be fine," I said. "I just felt faint for a moment."

"Hana, it'll be okay," Bayza said, stroking my hair. "Akmal is a good man, and it's easy to see that you two love each other. I just know you two will be so happy. And we'll always talk to each other and visit whenever we can. I know you'll visit us too."

"I thought you were angry with me. You've barely said two words to me all week," I said, almost grabbing her hand before remembering the henna.

"Of course I'm angry. You're my sister, like my twin. Selfishly I don't want you to leave me. But I am also happy for you because you and Akmal clearly love each other and are meant to be together." She smiled at me.

I forced a smile and stood again, pushing my anxiety down. "I know," I assured her. "It's just such a big change. It's almost too much to wrap my head around."

"You'll be okay," she encouraged me. "You're strong. If anything, we should be worried about Akmal. He's such a gentle soul. What will he do when he learns you aren't the kind, patient woman he thinks you are?"

She grinned mischievously as she said this, and I narrowed my eyes at her while Rabi rolled hers. "At least I can hide my sarcasm long enough to land a man," I retorted. "At this rate, Mom and Dad will have to marry you to a mule."

"Maybe a mule could control her," Rabi muttered. "Heaven knows Mom and Dad can't."

Bayza laughed. "I can't help it if I'm confident enough to express myself. Any man that marries me will have to accept that, or I'll die a spinster."

"Don't say that!" I protested. "You'll find someone."

"Of course, I will," she said. "I'm the only one who doesn't seem worried about that."

We continued to laugh and joke together well into the night, but I lay awake for a long time when the other two went to bed.

I was looking forward to marrying Akmal. I couldn't wait to be his wife before Allah and man. At the same time, the night that followed our marriage haunted me. The specter of my past seemed to hover just over me, corrupting every happy thought with a memory of Uncle Makhi.

***

The dawn arrived beautifully, painting the sky with gold, red, and pink. I watched from the roof of the tarma as the sun climbed slowly over the horizon. The soft coos of a morning dove were soon drowned by the bustle inside the house as the rest of my family woke up and busied themselves, preparing for the day ahead.

I heard my name called a few times but didn't descend yet. I realized this would be the last time I would ever sit on this roof and watch the sun rise over the desert horizon. It hit me suddenly that my childhood was over. The thought was a far sadder one than I thought it would be. Of course, my childhood had its good qualities, but it was coated forever with the blackness of my shame with Uncle Makhi. I never anticipated I would regret its end.

As I sat on the roof of my parents' house and watched the clear blue of the day drive away the red and gold of dawn, I knew I was wrong to feel that way. Whatever pain my childhood brought me, it was my childhood, and knowing that it existed now only as a memory was an overwhelming thought.

I heard someone climbing the ladder to the roof but didn't turn to see who it was. A moment later, my father sat next to me. He didn't say anything, nor did I. He only reached to me and grasped my hand.

We sat like that for a while as the rest of the family squabbled and hurried about in excitement for the big day. That last sunrise on the roof, holding my father's hand, is one of my favorite memories. It would be years before I truly believed this, but at that moment, I felt for the first time that everything really would be okay.

The night of the signing of the Nishan, I was dressed in a pure white nightdress embroidered with silver. My mother-in-law drew a circle on each palm and placed a coin in my hands. She then held my hands together so that the imprint of the coin was left on my palm. This was to protect me from the seven eyes. My sister and mother held a beautiful silk shawl over my head and grated a sugar cone over it. The bits of sugar fell around me like pure white snow, symbolizing the sweetness of life.

They sat me in a chair, soaking my feet in a basin filled with water and jasmine flowers. Their sweet smell permeated the air around me. In my hands, the women placed a mirror and the Quran. When all of this was finished, the Imam began to read. We all strained to hear his voice.

The Imam glanced up from his reading and smiled slightly, the only break in his formal demeanor during the ceremony. When it came time to recite our vows, he made the proper request of me and waited patiently.

I spoke clearly to be sure Akmal would hear my pledge through the closed door. "I, Hanen, offer you myself in marriage and in accordance with the instructions of the Holy Quran and the Holy Prophet, peace and blessing be upon him. I pledge, in honesty and with sincerity, to be for you a faithful and obedient wife."

My mother had silent tears of joy flowing down her face as she listened to me give myself to my husband.

All the women in the room were silent, straining to hear Akmal's pledge to me before Allah. "I, Akmal, in accordance with the instructions of the Holy Quran and the Holy Prophet, pledge, in honesty and sincerity, to be for you a faithful and helpful husband."

As tradition demands, the Imam asked us seven times if we accepted the other in marriage. When we both agreed, he presented the *Nikah*. As I signed the contract next to Akmal, I felt a burden lift from my soul even as another burden replaced it. I was his. I was not my own. May Allah bless us always. It was now that I finally saw Akmal. He came into the room and gently kissed me.

The Imam took the *Nikah* and made a show of examining the signatures. Then, he quite formally declared our marriage sealed.

Our gathered families cheered at the announcement from both sides of the door. When I saw him after the ceremony, Akmal wore a tailored suit that fit him immaculately. Despite my fear for the night to come, I felt a rush of pride, knowing it was my man who looked so handsome. He belonged all to me.

Three days later, we had our wedding party. I rented three beautiful dresses for it, a white, traditional-western gown and two beautiful, crystal-covered dresses, one green and one burgundy. I spent most of the day being pampered for the party. My hair took hours to arrange in an artful upsweep. When the hairdresser was done, my head felt like it weighed fifty pounds because of all the clips and products placed in my hair to hold the style in place. Then my sisters and I went to professionally get our nails and makeup done. I felt like a true Amiri that night. Never before had I felt so beautiful as I twirled around the dance floor with my husband, the sound of the drums beating all around us.

The party lasted well into the night. We gorged on quzi, dolma, biryani, heaps of fresh-baked samoon, and copious amounts of daheen and kanafeh for dessert. To wash it down, we enjoyed Grandma Fatima's special recipe for laban. Akmal and I alternated between sitting and standing close together and being pulled apart by warring clans of relatives.

So much went on at the party that I managed to avoid thoughts of the night to come and the fear and shame I knew would accompany it.

Eventually, however, the celebration dwindled to a close. Before I knew it, I embraced my mother and father and wished them a tearful goodbye, and Akmal and I were left alone.

He looked at me with affection and awkward anxiety but also with the lust that any married man has the right to feel for his wife. I smiled at him and turned so he could see my body in profile, demonstrating the willingness any wife should show her husband on their wedding night. Allah was gracious. I felt nothing but peace, and my husband was the only man in my head. Allah's greatest gift to me.

CHAPTER FIFTEEN

Mountain of Strength

Present Day, 35 years old, Alberta, Canada

On one of my walks to the park, I figured out the next step I needed to take in my healing journey. I had stopped to sit on a wooden bench near the lake to enjoy the afternoon sunshine on my face. I rooted around in the oversized bag I carried and pulled out a large zipper bag filled with stale bits of bread. I tossed a few pieces to the ducks waddling near me. Soon I was surrounded by geese, ducks, pigeons, and even a swan, fighting over the scraps I threw at them. I saved any leftover bread for this very purpose. This silly ritual relaxed me.

Suddenly, I felt a tug on the sleeve of my sweater. Startled, I saw a small girl, around five or six, standing at my feet. Her sparkling pink sneakers were toe to toe with my white ones.

"Hi. Can I help you feed the dwucks?" I smiled, finding her mispronouncing of ducks charming.

"I don't mind, but first, you need to find your mommy or daddy and ask them. We wouldn't want them to worry." I gently tell her.

"My daddy is right over thewe. He's weading a book, see." She pointed to a young man in his late twenties sitting on the bench about thirty feet from where I sat.

I was relieved to see he was closely watching the girl. He raised his hand and waved, letting me know he was there. I held up and pointed to the bread bag, silently asking if his daughter could feed the ducks. He nodded his head and returned to reading. Every few moments checking on the girl.

"Your daddy said it is okay." I handed her the bag, almost immediately realizing my mistake, when she unceremoniously dumped all the bread by her feet. Her delighted squeals as the birds flocked her way more than made up for the mistake.

She ran around, chasing the birds, her innocent laughter ringing out. Her joy was contagious. I smiled as she enjoyed her play, her long, dark hair swirling around her in the breeze.

It struck me that I wasn't so different when I was her age. I was a tiny girl with long dark hair who loved sparkly pink things, playing with the ducks, and twirling in circles around the tarma. That had been me before Mahki had stolen my joy and innocence.

And as I felt the righteous anger for his evil deeds burning through me, I knew exactly what I must do. Today, I would confront the monster from my past, my living nightmare. Today, I would confront Mahki.

I looked him up on social media before I called. He looked much the same as I remembered. There were a few more wrinkles, a few more pounds, and what little hair he had left was graying now, but the deceptively kind smile was the same as it always was, and his eyes were the same soft brown.

I was surprised to see he was married. His wife was pretty enough and seemed to actually like him. I'm not sure why this surprised me, but it did. I suppose because I hated him so much, it was a shock to see anyone feel differently. Then again, no one knew him like I did. The corners of my lips curled down in disgust.

He had children. Daughters. Two of them: one an infant, one barely more than two. I considered the timeline and decided he likely impregnated his wife before he married her. I laughed bitterly at that. He had been careful to avoid being trapped with one woman for decades, but he finally slipped.

I had only his photos and social media profile to go on, but he talked lovingly and at length about his wife and little girls. A part of me wanted to believe him, but I knew better. I thought about those poor girls without knowing who their father was, and my blood began to boil.

I shut my computer off, picked up my phone, and called him. I wondered if he would actually answer. He wouldn't recognize my number. Then again, he knew I lived in Canada, and how many other Canadian numbers would be calling him?

A second later, I heard him say, "Hello? Hanen?"

The sound of his voice was a punch to the gut. I had to sit down to keep from swaying on my feet. I didn't answer him until he asked again, "Hana, is that you?"

"Hello, Makhi," I said finally. My voice was far calmer than I was.

I wondered how long it would remain that way?"

"Hana!" Makhi said. "It's been so long! I haven't heard from you in ages."

"It has been a while," I agreed.

"That's so funny. I think your mom just left me a message the other day. I was just about to call her back."

You might not want to do that, I thought to myself. But I simply said, "Yes, I just spoke with her a few days ago."

"Oh good! I'm so glad. She worries about you, you know." "Yes, I know."

"Being a parent is wonderful, isn't it? You have this little, tiny life in your hands, and everything you do determines the kind of person they become. It truly is special."

"Yes," I said woodenly. "Special."

"You have children yourself, right? What are their names? Hamza, Hassan?"

"Hamsa and Hamid."

"Hamsa and Hamid. Those are good names. Strong names.

They'll grow up strong, just like their mother."

I didn't want to keep chatting. I called for one reason and one reason only, but I couldn't get the words out. I could only listen while he chatted about his wife and children and his new job as a consultant.

He seemed happy. He seemed so happy, and it infuriated me. What right did he have to be happy after causing me so much pain? What right did he have to a loving family when the memory of all he had done to me had eaten away at my soul like worms eat wood.

"How dare you?" My voice came out a menacing whisper that grew in volume and intensity.

I didn't plan on those words, but they popped out of my mouth without passing through my mind first. The young Hanen trapped in my soul was determined to be heard. This was her time for justice. Makhi was silent for a second, and when he spoke again, his voice had a touch of fear. "What? What did you say?"

"You heard me," I almost growled. "How dare you? How dare you be happy? How dare you have a family and children? Daughters, Makhi? You should never be left in a room with little girls, much less be a father to them."

There was a long pause, and for a brief moment, I feared he had hung up. Then he spoke again, shaky and thin, "Hana, I'm sorry. I'm not sure what's got you so upset."

"Yes, you are! You know *exactly* why I'm upset," I was on a roll now after years of suffering his abuse in silence. After years of blaming myself for his perversions, I was finally going to have my say, and only Allah himself would be able to stop me. "Tell me, Makhi, do they know? Do they know the monster that you are?"

I heard a sharp intake of breath over the phone and felt a rush of satisfaction, knowing I had rattled him. "What—what are you talking about?"

"Do they know you like touching little girls, Makhi? Do they know you're a child rapist? Do they know that pretty soon, they'll be the same age I was when you first shoved your disgusting tongue down my six-year-old throat? Does your wife know? Is she worried about her daughters, Makhi? She should be."

"Stop it!" he hissed, whispering to avoid being overheard.

"I am," I continued, ignoring him. "I'm very worried about them. I'll just bet your daughters love you. I'll bet you're the most amazing father ever in their eyes. I'll bet your wife's friends tell her how fortunate she is that her husband is so attentive to her and her children."

"Hana—"

"And you play that part so well, don't you? You probably smile and shrug and mumble something cute about how much Allah has blessed you, and you're just so grateful, and you don't understand why he bestows so many blessings on you, but he does, and you're just so grateful—"

"Hana, please! Stop it!"

"But deep down, Makhi? Deep down, you know better, and I know better. One day your demons will rise up again, and what happens then? What happens to that little girl who looks at you so lovingly now?"

"Hana, please, I'm begging you—"

"Begging me? Ha! I begged you, Makhi. Do you remember? Do you remember how I begged you to stop? I told you it hurt. I told you I didn't like this game. I told you I didn't like any of your games. I begged you with tears rolling down my face and blood running down my legs. Did that stop you? No, you just kept going. Ruining me. Ruining my childhood and ruining all that I could have been. It didn't matter that your niece was only six years old when you started."

"Hana, I'm sorry—"

"Six years old, Makhi!" Tears streamed down my face as I shouted at him. "I was six years old when you first touched me. Why? Why would you hurt a child like that? What could that possibly have done for you?"

He didn't answer at first, so I screamed into the phone. "Why?!

Answer me, you worthless piece of filth!"

"I don't know!" he shouted, choking on tears.

I listened as he wept, my mouth curling in contempt. "Really? You're going to cry? Your tears move me the same amount that my tears moved you while I begged you to stop hurting me. You are a vile piece of filth that deserves no mercy or compassion. So, for once in your miserable life, be a man, and own your actions. Tell. Me. WHY!"

"I don't know," he said, his voice shaky. "I—I always was like this. I try not to need it, but I can't help myself. I hate myself for it. I hated myself for touching you, Hana. I wanted bitterly for it to stop, but I couldn't—"

His voice choked off in a sob, and he wept wordlessly for a few more seconds.

I had no words. He had stolen my life from me, yet he saw himself as the victim? Was that how he truly saw himself? Helpless Makhi, a good person at heart but a slave to his uncontrollable fleshly urges. Can't you see he'd stop himself if he could?

"But you know, I'm better now," he said softly. "Ever since I met my wife, I don't think that way anymore. Thank Allah for her; she has cured me! I haven't looked at any other woman but her since we met. I swear to you, Hanen, I am a changed man. I love my daughters, and I would never hurt them. Please don't tell them of the past, Hanen, I beg of you."

He repeated himself for a minute before falling silent save for the occasional audible sniff or whimper. I had to cover my mouth to stifle a sudden urge to laugh. When I had myself under control, I said, "You know, when I was younger, I thought of you as this giant of a person, if not in stature, then in your ability to control a situation. I thought you were all-powerful because to little six-year-old Hanen, you held all the power. Now that I'm an adult, I realize just what a pathetic excuse you are for a man. You aren't powerful. You are a pathetic pig that abuses children because no one else can even look at you without laughing at how pathetic you are. Isn't that right, Uncle? Talking to you now, I realize how small you really are. You're not a slave, Makhi. You're a pig. And whatever guilt you might pretend to feel, you enjoy rooting in the muck as much as any pig."

"Yes," he choked. "Yes, you are right. I am a pig, a worthless pig."

"But you're happy to be, aren't you? As long as you keep getting away with it, you're happy to keep rooting in your muck."

"No! Hanen, I swear to you, I am a changed man—" "Does your wife know?"

A moment of silence. Then, "Hanen, please—"

"She should know, don't you think? She should know her daughters are being raised by a child rapist. I think that's information a mother should have."

"Hanen, I beg you; I promise you, I am not that man anymore. I love my daughters; I would never hurt them."

"But you loved me, didn't you? You used to tell me that all the time, remember? 'I love you, Hanen. I would never let anything happen to you.' Don't you remember saying that?"

"Hana, please, take my life if you must. Fly here and kill me. Have your father kill me. I'll allow it. Just please don't tell my wife. Don't tell my little girls."

"Don't you call them that!" I scream. "They are not *your* little girls! They are themselves. They have the unfortunate luck that you are their father, but they do not belong to you. You understand that, right now!"

"Yes, yes, I do. I know. I'm sorry."

"Speaking of my father, do you know why my mother called you?"

The silence on the other line was the sweetest revenge I could ever have had.

"Hana, no."

"Oh yes. That's right. Your older sister knows her younger brother raped her daughter and molested her for thirteen years. She wanted to tell my father, but I told her not to."

"Oh, Hana!" Makhi gushed in relief, "Thank you!"

"Shut up. I didn't do it for you. I did it for my father. He deserves to live the rest of his life in peace, never knowing the horrible things you did to me. I did it for your daughters. They seem to love you, and you seem to be behaving so far. But they aren't at that oh-so-enticing age of six. So, I doubt you would keep up the good behavior."

"I would never hurt my—"

"Shut up and listen. I'm going to tell you exactly how the rest of your life is going to be lived. I'm not going to stalk you. I'm not going to follow you. I'm not going to talk to you. I'm going to ignore you for the rest of my life. I'm going to move on. I won't celebrate when you die because it will have been so long since I thought about you that I won't even remember your name. You will become the little insignificant thing you are, and I will go forward with my life without a care in the world." I pause, enjoying the thought of forgetting him altogether.

"But my mother will never move on. Do you know how I know? Because I have children. I have a son and a daughter. If I ever found out that anyone hurt my babies, they would suffer unspeakably. I suggest you answer the phone the next time she calls. She will tell you she knows what you did to me, and I assure you, you would rather not have that conversation in person."

"Hana, no! What if—"

"What if she tells? Well, I imagine you'll be imprisoned at the very least. Then again, you know how exceedingly frowned upon raping children is. I can't imagine you'd survive very long in an Iraqi prison— if you even made it that far."

"Hanen, I beg of you—"

"There's nothing I can do, Makhi. Not that I would care to if I could. You're nothing to me anymore. But, like I said, if I wanted to do something, I couldn't. You know how strong-willed my mother is. You know how she is when she becomes fixated on something."

"Oh, God,"

"I rather doubt He's interested in helping you. But I'll offer you one piece of parting advice: From today onward, you are the best person who's ever lived."

"Yes, yes, of course—"

"Shut up. You are a saint. You are the most wholesome, perfect, supporting, utterly submissive husband and an outstanding role model for your two small children, who you never touch under any circumstances."

"No, never—"

"Do I have to have my father instruct you on the meaning of the phrase 'shut up'?"

"No, I'm sorry!"

"Good. Because I am quite sure that if you are ever anything other than this flawless model of mankind I've described, my mother will take great delight in telling my father all about how you tortured and abused me. Now you know how gentle my father is under ordinary circumstances. Still, I think you know he is quite different when it comes to his daughters."

"Yes, I know—"

"Considering how much trouble you have with the simple command to not speak, I have serious doubts, but no matter. Like I said, I'm going to forget you now. It's my mother you should concern yourself with. I would try to think how you will convince her you'll be perfect for the rest of your life."

"Hana, wait—"

"Now our roles are reversed. You will spend the rest of your life in misery, never knowing when the other shoe will drop. And I am going to live my life completely free of you. Goodbye, Mahki. Never speak my name again."

I hung up and let out a huge sigh. I felt as if the weight of the world had been lifted from my shoulders.

That was it.

It was over.

I was free.

Present Day, Office of Dr. Allison Peters

Today was my birthday. It had been exactly one year since that fateful night. I sat in Allison's office, amazed at the changes. In my hands, I held a card and a small box wrapped in brightly colored wrapping paper covered in skydivers and parachutes. I found it online and knew it was perfect for my adventurous therapist.

"Hi, Allison." I smiled as I held the gift out to her.

"Hanen, what's this?" She looked at the gift in surprise and started laughing when she realized what was on the wrapping.

"Oh my word, this is the best wrapping paper ever! Where in the world did you find it?"

"I came across it online. As soon as I saw it, I thought of you," I chuckled.

"The wrapping paper is so awesome; I almost don't want to open it!" She carefully unwrapped the cube, folded the paper, and put it in her desk drawer. Then she opened the box.

"You know me too well, Hanen!" she said as she held up the coffee mug and read it aloud, "Decaf? That's just one more issue we'll need to discuss." She laughed. "This is perfect. Thank you. But isn't it your birthday today? I should be giving you a gift."

"Today is exactly one year since I had my breakdown. This year, I have healed and grown so much. You have been a huge part of my healing journey. I wanted to thank you and commemorate the day positively."

"You humble me. But truly, Hanen, you did all the hard work. I simply listened and showed you the path. You should be very proud of yourself."

"I am. And on that note, I want to share a few things with you." I smiled excitedly.

"What have you been up to?" Allison arched her eyebrow jokingly.

"First, I called and confronted Makhi about how he abused me. It was the most freeing experience. At first, I had difficulty getting the words out, but once I started speaking, I couldn't stop. By the end of the call, he was afraid of me. I walked away feeling like I reclaimed my power!"

"Hanen, that is amazing! Confronting your abuser took a lot of courage. I'm glad you were able to find healing in it. I think it is important to be able to say the things you could never say while you were in the midst of the abuse. Many victims can't confront their abusers in real life because it would be unsafe, they have passed away, or any number of other reasons. For those victims, I advise them to write a letter to the person that hurt them. After they say everything they need to say, I tell them to burn, shred, or destroy it in some way as a symbol of closing that part of their past and walking in their healing. You may find that you must confront him again if you have to deal with more as you heal. I want you to know that you can write one of these letters anytime. Healing is very rarely done in a straight line. It is more like a spiral circling in on itself until you reach the very center of the issues. This is normal. Our brains only allow us to handle so much at a time. They are always protecting us the best that they can. So, if the time comes and you find yourself recircling an issue you thought you had completely healed from, don't be discouraged. Instead, know that your brain is saying you are ready to handle a deeper level of healing."

"I'm glad you told me that because sometimes I get frustrated when triggered by the smell of laban or crying when I see a little girl running carefree and innocent through the park. It's good to know that I'm not doing something wrong. That this is just a part of the process."

"Healing takes time, but that is okay. You are a strong woman who likes to get things done and check off your to-do list. But Hanen, remember that this journey is not a chore that you can tick off a list. You can't rush it. It takes time. It takes learning to give yourself the grace to be imperfect. And it takes learning to love yourself exactly as you are, no matter where you are on the journey." Allison handed me the tissue box sitting next to me on the table. I had thought for sure I would make it through this session without crying. Oh well, at least these were good tears.

After I dabbed my eyes, I gave Allison a peaceful smile, "I've also made two decisions I want to share with you. As you know, I have been studying to become a teacher here in Canada. But I've decided that I want to change the focus of my studies. Instead, I want to become a therapist and help other women and girls who have been abused to heal.

There aren't a lot of resources for women to use back in Iraq and other middle eastern countries. So, my second decision is that I am going to write a book to share my story and the journey I've taken to heal. Hopefully, I can help women who don't have access to the resources I have here in Canada."

"Wow! I am excited to hear this. I would love to help you in any way that I can. I'm here for you as you start this new journey."

Later, after the kids were in their rooms listening to their music and studying, I turned on my computer, opened a new document, and began to write. "When I was a young girl of only six…."

Here is the list of names of people who appeared in this book.

Hanen= teller of story

Bayza =younger sister

Akhmal=husband

Mahki=uncle who abused her

Arif= uncle

Therapist=Allison

Older sister=Shameera

Mother=Lana

Father= Ayad

Sister= youngest Zayna

Grandmother/father's side=Khadija

Grandmother/mother's side=Fatima

Best friend in Iraq=Sama

Best friend in Canada= Allisya

Son= Hamed

Daughter= Hamsa

University crush=Ali

Look for Book Two of Hanen's Story. Coming Soon

The End

Shatha would like to thank Kristine Skiff and her company, **Gift An Author Publishing** for telling Hanen's story in English and advising on other aspects of publishing. Not My Sin will soon be available in Arabic. Look for it on Amazon or your favorite book site.

www.ingramcontent.com/pod-product-compliance
Lightning Source LLC
Chambersburg PA
CBHW020034310726

48970CB00007B/2253